FURY AT
SWEETWATER PASS

Also by Lee Martin

Shadow on the Mesa

Fast Ride to Boot Hill

The Last Wild Ride

The Grant Conspiracy: Wake of the Civil War

Fury at Cross Creek

In Mysterious Ways

Revenge at Rawhide

The Maverick Gun

The Darringer Brothers Series:

Trail of the Fast Gun

Trail of the Long Riders

Trail of the Hunter

Trail of the Circle Star

Trail of the Restless Gun

Trail of the Dangerous Gun

and coming soon…

The Lone Rider

FURY AT
SWEETWATER PASS

LEE MARTIN

VACA MOUNTAIN PRESS
Vacaville, California, U.S.A.

Vaca Mountain Press
Paperback ISBN 13: 978-1-952380-26-6
Kindle ISBN 13: 978-1-952380-27-3

Also available in
Large Print ISBN 13: 978-1-952380-28-0

Library of Congress Catalog Card Number: 92-93577

Interior design by Eddie Vincent, ENC Graphic Services
Cover design by Deirdre Wait for ENC Graphic Services
Cover images: landscape by Deirdre Wait; cowboy on horse © Getty Images

Published by Vaca Mountain Press

Visit Lee Martin Westerns on Facebook.

To all of my wonderful family,
and in the fond memory of
my beloved mother,
my beautiful sister Arlene,
our rough riding brothers,
and for Jim Liontas.

FURY AT SWEETWATER PASS

ONE

Settled around the campfire, the weary cowhands listened with pleasure to the sweet strains of Tyler Sinclair's harmonica until pink-faced Shorty was called on to read from his dime novel. The words of the slender book would soon turn Tyler's world upside down.

Tyler lay back on his saddle, sliding his harmonica into his vest pocket. His reddish brown hair was damp under his black Stetson. A day's growth of beard darkened his weathered face, and his gray-blue eyes burned from the New Mexico dust.

Tyler, Shorty, and the five other men were dirty, but Shorty's readings were important and would help them sleep.

Shorty cleared his throat. "This one's called *The Town Tamer.* Its hero is supposed to be a dead shot who never misses. In fact, he's even better than Tyler here."

"Who is this dude?" one of the men asked.

"Name's Ethan Mandell."

Tyler went as stiff as a board. His wide mouth tight and dry, he rose to his elbow, listening intently.

"Go on, Shorty," someone said.

The men spread out on the hard ground near the crackling fire of stinking chips. Staring at the starry sky, they watched the swing of the Big Dipper around the North Star, the cowboy's clock. Soon it would be midnight, and it was plenty cold. The only sounds were the distant herd, an occasional snort from the remuda, and the snore of the cook under the chuck wagon.

"Well, sir," Shorty said, sitting cross-legged, "it goes like this. 'Ethan Mandell had just killed another man. He stood in the streets of Tucson with his smoking six-shooter in his big hand, his star glistening on his vest. His dark-red hair was long to his big shoulders. He knew no fear.' "

As Tyler listened to the saga of the heroic lawman's taming of the West, his heart beat in painful rhythm and his skin itched as if covered with ants. His blanket was so hot that he pushed it away, and he loosened his red bandanna.

The novel carried the hero through many gunfights and death-defying feats throughout southern Arizona Territory.

By the end of the story, Shorty's voice was hoarse. " 'His work done, Ethan Mandell will move north to take up the badge of a United States deputy marshal in the new state of Colorado at bloody Sweetwater, near Sweetwater Pass in the eastern foothills of the Rockies. Someday, there will be a bullet in his back, and the West will lose one of the greatest town tamers that ever lived.' "

"That was a good one," one of the men said. "Sure made it sound like he was right here with us. But I ain't never heard of 'im. You figure he really is that tough?"

"I heard of 'im once when I was over in Tombstone," another man said. "They say he's meaner than an old mosshorn in the brush. They figure he's killed a couple dozen men."

"Hey, Shorty," a hand mumbled as he rolled over, "don't forget to pick up another one of them stories."

Tyler watched the other men curl up in their blankets. One of the night riders was out there singing with a voice like a frog. A coyote howled in the far spread of the prairie. It was June of 1880 in New Mexico Territory, and the men had been rounding up from brush country. Their chaps were scraped and their clothes were torn, with some of their skin still up in the bluffs.

Riding in pairs, they had watched for Mescalero Apaches. So far, they were all alive, but they ached so bad that they were certain their rumps were worn through the skin and that their bones would never again pull free of their flesh. Every man's five or six mounts had scrapes and bruises, and some were lame.

Shorty yawned and started to put the dime novel away, rolling it up like a small newspaper, but Tyler held out his hand for it. The little man was reluctant, but handed it over.

"All right, Tyler, but stick it in my war bag when you're through. And you'd better get some sleep. We're up in a couple of hours."

Tyler's damp hands closed on the novel. He leaned forward on his elbow toward the firelight. His blue linen shirt and black leather vest were hot, and his Stetson suddenly felt tight around his thick hair.

The cover of the novel had a drawing of a big man with a hooked nose, fierce eyes, and a handlebar mustache that drooped down to his square jaw. In his hand was a revolver, and it pointed toward the reader. Tyler swallowed hard. Was this man his father? Shorty arose from his blankets. "Hey, don't crumple that up. I paid a whole dollar for it over in Socorro."

3

"I'll give you five."

Forehead wrinkled, wide mouth twisted, Shorty considered the worry written across Tyler's dark face. He sat up slowly. "You got a reason?"

"This could be my father. At least, it's the same name as his, and I ain't never run across it before." Shorty's pinched face caught the glow of the firelight as he turned fully about. Then he wiped his mouth and settled down on his elbow. "Glory be. Just give me the dollar I paid for it."

Tyler reached in his leather poke for his last silver dollar, which he handed over. "Thanks."

"You gonna be headin' for Colorado, then?"

"I don't know. He ran out on us afore I was born." Tyler leaned back on his saddle and stared at the novel in his hand. Shorty was his partner, and he couldn't help confiding in someone for the first time.

"They were married only a few weeks when he killed my mother's brother in a gambling fight. He took off right after and was never heard from again."

"Was it a fair fight?"

"The law said it was, but my mother said he was good-for-nothing, a gambler and gunman. All I heard when I was growing up, back in Kentucky, was how bad he was. And Ma never looked one bit sorry he was gone."

"Your ma still alive?"

"No. She got him declared dead and the marriage annulled when I was seven, and she married Walden Sinclair, a lawyer with a lot of money. I got adopted and my name was changed. She died of a fever when I was twelve."

"Sinclair still alive?"

Tyler shrugged. "I don't know. I took off when I was fourteen."

"You didn't get along?"

"Never had a chance. I worked in his law office, but he was too busy to even talk to me. But her family and his were all down on me, saying I had bad blood. And I had cousins that kept harassing me. One day, three of them came after me behind the house and started beating on me with clubs. But I beat the tar out of all three. After that, I knew I was in for it, so I just took off."

"Where'd you go?"

"I joined the Army. Lied about my age."

"Did you see action in the war?"

"More than I want to remember. Petersburg was the worst. My outfit had split up and I was attached to General Grant. In three days, we lost over eight thousand men—killed, wounded, or missing. I was covered with other men's blood."

"Must have been tough. I'm older'n you, so I was in it from the start. But I was fightin' for the South. Don't matter now, I reckon. But I never got that far north."

"I sure grew up fast."

"And you never went home? Never wrote?"

"Never went back. But I wrote Sinclair once. Last year, as a matter of fact. It was after we went to that prayer meeting on the trail. All of a sudden I got mighty lonesome for home. But I never got an answer."

"All this time you never said nothin' to us guys."

"I reckon I wanted to forget."

"So, how old are you now?"

"I'll be twenty-nine on the Fourth of July." Tyler held

the novel's cover to the light and stared at the man's face. "I wonder if he really looks like this."

"You got to know, Tyler, that a lot of these writers never even seen the men they write about. You think they ever saw Billy the Kid? Or Wild Bill Hickok? Well, could be they never met this Ethan Mandell."

"I always thought he was probably dead."

"Tyler, you've got to give him a chance to speak for hisself. You owe him that much."

Tyler put the novel into his saddlebag, and then he lay back and stared at the stars, his eyes burning. "Shorty, I've hated him all my life, the way he ran out on us and never wrote. But I tried to forget about it."

"And now?"

"You were right. I've got to find out for myself." Tyler could hear another night rider singing in a clear tenor, and he knew he had to sleep, because his own turn was coming. But all he could think of was Colorado and Sweetwater Pass.

"You know," Shorty said in a low voice, his eyes closed, "I think you must've been mighty lonely all these years. You should have got married."

"It's not for me."

"Well, I'm gonna miss you, pardner."

*   *   *

And so it was that Tyler left the outfit and headed north for the eastern foothills of the Rocky Mountains. He rode a black gelding, his best swimming horse. His yellow slicker and fat bedroll were behind the cantle, over his saddlebags.

Every night on the trail, he would sit and read the novel. Often he shook his head at the extravagance of the writer. He wondered if Ethan Mandell was really anything like that, or if he was the useless gambler described by other people.

When he entered Colorado, he stopped at Pueblo, a busy railroad town. A narrow-gauge train was at the depot, its smoke rising above the buildings. In the center of the wide street was a giant tree, two ropes hanging from one hardy limb. The trunk had to be twenty to thirty feet around.

"You missed the hangin'," a stout little man told Tyler, his beard twitching. "Two at one time. A real sight."

Tyler shrugged and turned and walked to the Stockgrowers National Bank, where he cashed a draft from his former employer. He refused greenbacks and insisted on hard money. His wages for the last three months amounted to almost a hundred dollars.

The gray, balding banker watched as Tyler filled his poke. "Where you headed now, young feller?"

"Sweetwater Pass."

"That's not such a good idea. They're killin' each other off up there. I hear they hired Ethan Mandell to clean it up, but they'll kill him, too."

Tyler left town at once. He wanted to see Ethan Mandell while the man was alive. Filled with hate and curiosity, he couldn't turn back.

He headed for the foothills, where the trail to Sweetwater led through yellow pines and shimmering aspens. Far beyond, snow-covered mountains thrust their peaks into the clouds.

Yellow and purple wildflowers were scattered on the slopes in the lush green grass. The air was cold but crisp, and filled with the scent of honeysuckle. Willows and cottonwoods, noisy with chickadees and magpies, shaded the creeks where fragile ferns reached to the banks. He saw tracks of deer, bobcat, and bear.

A crooked sign pointed the way to Sweetwater Pass. As he rode onto a plateau that afternoon, he saw the land open before him like a shining, rolling spread of green satin for miles in every direction.

And then he heard a rifle shot ahead and to the south. As he continued riding, he saw the buzzards circling in that direction. The black, ugly creatures sailed on the wind, waiting to pounce on some carcass out there in the deep grass.

Curious, Tyler rode off the wagon road until he came over a small rise. There, flat on his face, lay the body of a youth with a blotch of blood on the back of his blue shirt. His hair was blond, his hat way off in the rocks. A sorrel gelding grazed nearby, reins trailing.

Tyler shook his head as he looked around at the distant pines and the vast expanse of valley in all directions. He circled the area, even venturing into the pines, but there were no tracks. The shot could have come from anywhere. He dismounted and knelt by the dead man and turned him over.

The victim was in his late teens, clean-shaven, with blue eyes staring at the sky. Tyler closed the eyes with his hand. He found a leather poke in the boy's pocket. It contained a few dollars and a bill of sale for some beef and hides made out to the Rollins Freighting Company in Sweetwater.

Rising with the poke and papers in his left hand, Tyler pushed his hat back in thought. If he buried him here and now, some mother would never be sure her son was dead.

The youth had probably died only an hour ago, at about the time Tyler had heard the rifle shot. He started to kneel down to replace the poke and papers when he thought he heard hoofbeats. He rose again, turned, and saw a bay mare on a far rise, first at a lope and then suddenly at a gallop.

Tyler stood ready, hand near his holster. The mare slowed to a trot and then a walk. The rider held a rifle across the pommel. As the rider came closer, Tyler was surprised.

Astride the mare was a young woman in her early twenties, golden hair flying long and lustrous in the sunlight. She wore some kind of riding skirt and a heavy buckskin coat with a fringe, a man's hat pulled down tight with a chin strap, and a gun belt strapped around her waist with a sidearm. As she came closer, he saw that her small nose tipped up slightly, but she was about as pretty a woman as he had ever seen.

She kept her rifle across the pommel, and as she reined to a halt and stared down at the body, her face twisted in sudden horror.

"Jody!" she cried. And then she aimed her weapon at Tyler. "You did this! And you were robbing him!"

"I just got here, and I was looking to see who he was."

"Stand back and put your hands up."

Tyler dropped the poke and papers on the body, then stepped back with his hands at his sides. She glared at him, then swung down from the saddle, keeping her rifle on him.

"Drop your gun belt."

"No, ma'am, I ain't gonna do that."

Rifle still pointed at him, she knelt, her free hand shaking as she grabbed the boy's shirt. She shook him, stared, then sobbed, choking on her horror. She shoved the poke and papers into her coat pocket. After a moment she stood up, tears in her large blue-green eyes.

The rifle still pointed at him, she glared at Tyler, her face dark with fury. And she backed away.

"You did this."

Tyler shook his head. "No, ma'am. Like I told you, I just got here."

"That's what *you* say! I'm Celia Rollins and that's my brother, Jody, and I say you killed him." Color danced on her face, and it was obvious she didn't believe in his innocence, and didn't *want* to believe in it.

"Well, ma'am, if you're agreeable, we'll take him on in to town and you can tell that to the marshal." She stood tense, her rifle still aimed at him. Then, as he knelt to try to lift the body, she caught up the sorrel.

He managed to get the body on the saddle and tie it down, then cover it with a tarp from her bedroll. The girl swung onto her bay, keeping her rifle on him. Distrust was written all over her face.

Heading west once more with the sorrel on a lead and the girl riding behind him, Tyler came upon a big, twenty-foot wide, deep and rushing white-water creek that flowed east toward the plains. Cattle grazed in all directions. He rode on the south side of the creek and into twilight as he saw the shape of the town far ahead. It straddled the deep water and spread north and south with a wooden bridge in between. There, the creek was just as wide, but apparently deeper.

The chill he felt was more than from the cold of night. He wasn't thinking about the body or the pretty girl riding behind him. At any moment, he might meet the man who had deserted him and his mother. Once, when she was getting dressed to wed Walden Sinclair, she had taken him aside and said:

"It's a new life. Our family has position, but Mr. Sinclair has money. You'll have everything you always wanted, including a father."

"What about my real father?"

She had snapped at him, "Don't you ever ask about him again! I told you, Ethan Mandell was a bad man and he never cared about us. As far as we're concerned, he's dead."

Grim with the memory, and his heart rattling around in his chest, he rode along the creek bank. He saw an old, broken wagon half out of the swirling water. He rode to where the wooden bridge crossed the wide creek to the north side, then reined his black to a halt.

He could imagine the music and laughter from the saloons and dance halls north of the bridge. From the windows, flickering lights fell on hitching rails lined with cow ponies and mules.

"What are you stopping for?" Celia shouted.

Tyler turned in the saddle, rode back toward her, and tossed the lead rope into her startled grasp. "Look, ma'am, go ahead and shoot if you want, but I'm going to the livery to take care of my horse."

Turning south, he immediately saw the livery barn and corrals on his left, and across the street, a building with a sign: U.S. Marshal. Dim lights were behind the inside shutters of the two front windows.

As he rode up to the livery, she passed him, the sorrel trailing with her brother's body. She was sitting stiff and angry in the saddle, but Tyler didn't have time to think about her problems.

He had enough of his own.

Mouth dry as bone, he turned into the barn where oil lamps burned on the walls on each side. Stalls lined the left wall, and there were bunks on the right where saddles and other gear were stacked. Above was a huge loft, and in back was a big window with the beam for hauling in hay.

A skinny black man came forward, cigar in his teeth, his smile a welcome sight. "Hello, mister. What can I do for you? I'm Paxton, and I look after this here barn for Mr. Filer."

"Tyler Sinclair. Need to put up my horse and get some sleep."

"Take that last bunk over there. One dollar for you and your horse. Some oats in that barrel. Now, that sure looked like Celia Rollins leading her brother's horse."

Tyler dismounted. "Found her brother out in the valley. Shot in the back."

"Sorry to hear that. Afore the marshal came a few months back, we was finding dead men once a month. Some were hanged by the vigilantes."

"But why kill that boy?"

"There's two freight companies fightin'. Rollins on this side, Crocker on the north. Too much gold and silver comin' down from the pass, and heaps of machinery and supplies goin' up. Both companies want all the business, and gettin' rid of Jody Rollins sure helps Crocker."

"Nice folks around here."

Paxton nodded. "The Filers are the leading citizens on the south side, and when they heard a deputy marshal was comin' to Sweetwater, they put out the money to build that jailhouse, just for show."

"Who's the marshal?"

"Ethan Mandell. Toughest man I ever met. Got here a couple of months ago. I work for him as a part-time deputy."

Tyler felt a tightness in his chest. Any moment now, he would meet the man who might well be his father. His face was burning and damp. He was so deep in thought that Paxton's next words startled him:

"I'll put up your horse. You go find the marshal and tell him what happened."

Tyler thanked him and paid the dollar. He left the barn and stood in the chill of night. Tense, he rested his hand on his Army Colt in its cut-down holster that rested low on his right hip. In his left hand, his Winchester was balanced. Across the way, the jailhouse was silent.

He looked south along the nearly empty street. There were shops, a hotel and a saloon, a stage depot, a freight office with corrals behind it, a bank, and all the usual markings of a respectable town. Only a few horses were at the railings, and he saw no sign of the woman and her brother, but now he was looking for Ethan Mandell.

Drawing a deep breath, he knew he could wait no longer, and he started to cross toward the jail. It was then that he saw movement down the street to his left, shadows in the moonlight.

A big, husky man was walking toward him along the boardwalk, his steps barely audible. Tyler saw the gleam of a star and caught his breath.

But upon the roof of a store across the street, a rifle barrel glistened, and it was aimed at the back of Ethan Mandell.

TWO

*T*yler froze for just a second while the lawman walked toward him in the moonlight. Tyler's thumb was on the hammer of his six-gun even as he swept it from his holster. From the corner of his eye, he saw the lawman pulling his revolver. But Tyler had already hit his mark.

The man on the roof cried out. His rifle rolled down into the alley. Then he doubled up and crashed into the alley with a loud thud. Tyler felt the hurt and cold with the pain of killing another man.

The lawman spun about and charged across the street while Tyler slowly holstered his weapon. He stared at the big man's back. Even in the moonlight, he could see the long, graying red hair, the big shoulders, and catlike movement.

Ethan Mandell was wearing a brown leather vest and two sidearms, one still in his hand. He knelt in the alley to confirm that the man was dead. Then, holstering his gun, he rose and turned to walk back into the moonlight.

The two men faced each other in the street, the lawman with curiosity, Tyler with wild anxiety.

Ethan had a hooked nose and strong features, much stronger than Tyler's, above his drooping handlebar mustache. About fifty, he had a square jaw and wide mouth, but there was no other clear resemblance. Tyler was six feet tall, but Ethan was several inches over that. The lawman matched the drawing on the novel, but was bigger and bolder in appearance.

"Ethan Mandell, son, and I thank you."

Tyler tried to swallow, but his throat was too dry. His heart was beating so fast that he feared it would break.

"Tyler Sinclair."

"Glad you were here, Tyler."

Tyler tensed, but realized his name meant nothing to the man. The real Ethan Mandell likely didn't know that Tyler's mother had annulled the marriage to wed Sinclair. Nor would he know she had died.

The lawman offered his hand. With a prickly pain in his chest, Tyler reached to take it. Ethan's hand was strong and hard, bigger than Tyler's. His firm grip sent a shattering shock all the way up Tyler's arm. He drew back, his voice husky.

"You know who that was tried to kill you?"

"Seen 'im over on the north side at Crocker's saloon. Recognized the rope burn on his neck."

Faces were at the curtains of many buildings, but they seemed afraid to come out. Three men appeared from the saloon across the street, and Ethan commissioned them to take care of the body. Then he turned to Tyler once more as onlookers began to go back into the buildings.

"You saved my life, son."

"I was coming through the valley this afternoon and heard a

rifle shot." Tyler thought this was a good time to make his case. "I went off the trail and found a dead man out on the flats. Bullet in his back. Didn't see no signs."

"I know. I saw Celia Rollins taking her brother to the undertaker. She thinks you done it."

"He was shot with a rifle," Tyler said, handing over his Winchester. "Take a whiff. It's been oiled and cleaned for a week and not fired since."

Ethan sniffed the rifle, then returned it. He seemed satisfied, and he pulled his hat down tight as he spoke: "I never seen a man draw so fast. I figured you was goin' for me, and you're the first to outdraw me." Tyler was surprised at the pride he felt at the man's praise. He told himself to take it slow. He knew nothing of his father beyond years of anger and the pages of a dime novel filled with impossible deeds. And this man might not even be the same Ethan Mandell.

"How'd you get so fast with a gun?" Ethan asked.

"I had a hankering to win all them shooting contests. And with some practice, I never lost a one."

"Ever kill a man before?"

"Yeah, down in Texas when we hunted rustlers. And back in the war. Don't like it much. I'd rather be shooting to win."

"Contest comin' up here on the Fourth of July. They're givin' away a Winchester rifle."

"Now that I would sure want to win."

"Over there on the right, that's Filer's Bank. Up the street just past it, that's Filer's Hotel, which has the best food in town. You can get steak and all the trimmings for two bits. And on the left, that's the Rollinses' freight office."

"I hear they have competition."

"Yeah, from Crocker over on the north side. Big business up at the pass, but the Rollins outfit was losin' shipments right and left afore I got here. Masked riders turned the wagons over, sometimes in the creek. Just the same, she won't quit."

"She?"

"Yeah, Maggie Rollins, and her daughter, Celia. Maggie's husband was killed ridin' by hisself up to the pass, maybe a year afore I came. He was robbed of his gold watch and everything, but I don't figure that was the motive. Now, with Jody gone, there's just the two of 'em."

"Women running a freight outfit?"

"Don't make sense," Ethan growled. "And they're just gonna get hurt. But that Celia, she's one tough little woman. Tryin' real hard to take her father's place."

"Yeah, she sure threw down on me."

"Don't let it bother you, son. She's never trusted any man around here. Except maybe Pete Filer, the banker's son. He's been courtin' her right regular."

Tyler was trying to see the color of the man's eyes, but it was too dark.

They walked up to the freight office, behind which were corrals and wagons. Lights burned around the heavy curtains. Ethan knocked, and the curtains moved to throw light on him. A well-rounded woman unbarred and opened the door. She had blonde hair done up in a bun and was about fifty. Her cheeks were rosy, her brown eyes bright. She had a cute face and was unusually feminine.

Tyler glanced at Ethan. The lawman was gazing at her as if he were in a trance. It was then that Tyler discovered with anxiety that Ethan had the same gray-blue eyes as his.

17

She frowned as they tipped their hats. "Well, Marshal, I heard some shots up the street."

"Someone was takin' a potshot at me, but Tyler Sinclair, this young fellow, he got 'im first. Tyler, this here's Maggie Rollins."

She smiled and extended her hand. "Welcome, Tyler."

"Uh, Maggie, is Celia here?"

"No, she rode out to meet Jody. He's been making a deal with one of the ranchers. They should have been back by now. Is something wrong?"

Ethan swallowed. His face lost color and his mustache twitched.

Maggie's face darkened. "Come inside, Marshal."

When they were inside the cluttered office, she sat down at the desk and gripped some papers as if they gave her comfort. Behind her was a long hallway that could lead to the corrals, and on each side was a door closed to back rooms, apparently their living quarters. She had her gaze fixed on Ethan.

"What is it, Marshal?" There was terror in her dark eyes.

Ethan stood by her desk while Tyler waited near the door. The lawman's face was tight with dread as he spoke.

"Tyler here found Jody out in the valley. Shot in the back. Celia has him over at the undertaker's."

His words hit her like a fist. She reeled and looked away. Then, covering her face with her hands, she placed her elbows on the desk and leaned forward and sobbed.

Ethan looked helpless, his face strained. His hand reached to touch her shoulder, but never quite made it.

"Maggie, I'm sure sorry."

She choked on her sobs, then drew back, face red, and with tears in her eyes. She was still shaking, but this time with anger.

"I know darn well who done it—Wiley Crocker, that's who! He's been plenty mad ever since we got them Studebaker wagons and beat him up to the pass. He takes twice as long with his big ole heavy ones. Back when he heard we was gettin' them wagons, he killed my husband, thinkin' we'd just quit. But we showed 'im. And now he got Jody, my boy."

"You don't know it's Crocker," Ethan said. "Who else would want to stop your wagons? Your men say the riders were always masked."

"It's got to be Crocker," she insisted. "All them gunmen do is unhitch the team and turn the wagons over a bluff or into the creek. Who'd want to do that except Crocker? And he killed my husband because he wouldn't give up. And now he's murdered the last man in our family."

Ethan sighed and shifted his weight.

They heard running boots on the boardwalk, then saw the door jerked open. Standing in the lamplight was Celia Rollins, her pretty face red and dirty, her eyes wild under long lashes. Flaxen hair was spilling from under her wide-brimmed man's hat. She wasn't very tall, but the anger in her face made her sky high.

"Marshal, why don't you arrest this man?"

"Celia," her mother said softly, "please come in and shut the door."

"But Jody's over at the undertaker's and—"

Her mother rose up a few inches. "Shut the door." Frantic, Celia came inside and closed the door behind her. She was breathing fast and trying to be calm.

"Ma, I found this man with Jody right after he was killed. I figure he was about to rob him."

19

Ethan tugged at his mustache. "Now, Miss Celia, you don't really know that. Tyler here says he heard the shot and went looking, and he found the body, that's all. His rifle hadn't been fired. You told me it was a rifle you heard, and he says the same."

"But he looked like he was robbing Jody."

Tyler shook his head. "I told you, I was looking to see who he was."

Celia glared at Tyler, and he was conscious that she would barely come to his shoulder. He was suddenly aware, too, of his unshaven face and dirty clothes. And of her sharp tone of voice.

"Ma, we got to do something."

"The marshal's in charge, Celia. We know it's the Crocker outfit, not this poor young stranger. Now sit down."

Celia sat down on a chair, her face still red. She turned and glared at Tyler as she struggled not to cry. "How do we know you didn't do it? You got a cut-down holster and it's tied down, just like them fellers on the north side. You look like a hired gun to me." Maggie shook her head. "Don't mind Celia, Mr. Sinclair. She's got a bit of a temper. Especially when somethin' happens she can't do nothin' about."

Ethan pulled his hat down tight. "Well, we'll be goin'."

"Marshal," Maggie said, rising slowly, "you know Crocker's behind this and half of everything else around here."

Ethan shrugged and opened the door. "We got no proof."

"I'll find proof," Celia said. "One way or the other."

Tyler paused and gazed down at her. He couldn't tell if her large eyes were blue with flecks of green or the other way around. They were like crystal, and brimming with the tears she was fighting.

"If you're not a hired gun, why are you here?" Celia asked him. "You sure don't look like a miner. Or a merchant, either. And if you were ridin' the grub line, you wouldn't be in town."

Maggie moved around to put her hand on Celia's shoulder.

"She'll apologize tomorrow, Mr. Sinclair."

Celia abruptly turned her back, her hands over her face. Both women were badly shaken, but Maggie followed them to the door, her face streaked with tears. "Thanks for coming, Ethan. I'm going over to see my boy."

"You keep your doors locked tonight. You and Celia could be next."

"They wouldn't kill a woman."

"Don't bet on it. And you tell Celia no more ridin' out by herself."

"We'll have the funeral tomorrow. Will you be there?"

Ethan nodded and followed Tyler outside. After a few steps, Tyler took a deep breath and muttered, "That Celia's one angry young woman."

"It's because she can't prove nothin', and she's lost her father and brother. But she may have a point about one thing. Why did you come to Sweetwater?"

Tyler's throat was so dry that he could hardly talk.

"I was tired of herding cattle, and I wanted to find a new line of work, that's all. Heard this was a boomtown. Even thought I might file for a homestead, get a patent, and start my own herd."

"Most all the land's been filed on around here. The ranchers even have their men file so they can spread out."

Tyler wanted to change the subject. "That Maggie, she likes you."

21

Ethan shrugged. "I can't do nothin' about it. Besides, Percy Filer's camped on her doorstep, and I figure he'd take good care of her. He's got manners and a lot of money."

Tyler stiffened. If Ethan was his father, he didn't know he was a free man. But Tyler had no urge to ask him, because he was beginning to think that this man, who showed compassion and intense strength, could not be the useless father who had deserted him.

"You see me tomorrow, son, and let me know if you want a job. I need someone to watch my back."

"You don't even know me."

"I know men. And you saved my life."

"It was a reflex action."

"No, it was more than that."

Tyler was uncomfortable. He knew he had a gift with a gun, but he had no urge to gain a reputation. And he would never wear a badge, even for this man.

"Think on it, son. And if you're hungry, go on down to the hotel."

*　　*　　*

After a good meal, Tyler went back to the livery and turned into his blankets. He fell asleep with his six-gun on his belly, even while Paxton kept talking about the trouble in Sweetwater.

In the morning, Tyler awakened to the click of a hammer and found a gun in his face, the barrel gleaming with certain death. A tightness gripped his belly under his blankets, where he held his own weapon. He looked up at the thin-faced youth in a pin-striped suit and narrow-brimmed hat. He was barely twenty, but his attitude was that of a curious snake.

Suddenly, the man laughed, withdrew his gun, and shoved it into the holster under his coat. His eyes were dark, and his mouth twisted open around crooked teeth and under a thin black mustache.

"Sure did scare you, didn't I?"

Tyler sat up, his six-gun in his hand. He shoved his blankets aside and leveled his weapon as he stood up to face the youth. Anger hot on his face, he cried, "I oughta blow your head off."

"Hey, I was just funnin'."

Slowly, Tyler holstered his weapon. "Who the devil are you?"

"Slap Dooley."

"Tyler Sinclair, and I don't like your sense of humor."

They were alone in the livery. Tyler was having a hard time being angry at this man with an easy manner, and he turned to roll up his blankets.

Slap stood around watching. "Them's sure fancy boots. I bet you had 'em made for you, huh? Musta cost twenty dollars or more. And that there Stetson musta cost as much."

"Yeah. Ain't you got nothing better to do?"

"I'm goin' to a funeral."

"Jody Rollins?"

"Yeah. I didn't like 'im much, but ain't much else to do around here."

"Maybe you knew the man who tried to kill the marshal."

"Oh, yeah—Luke Smithers. I seen him around, but they already buried him. All the fancy folks will be at this one. And some pretty girls."

Tyler went over to the washbowl. While washing his face, he felt the growth of several days of beard.

As Slap left, Paxton came wandering inside and he glared after the youth. "There's a good-for-nothin'."

"Does he work for anyone?"

"No, but his brothers work for Crocker. Three of the meanest hombres you ever saw. Hop, Skip, and Jump, if you can believe how they're called. You can tell Jump by his beard. Skip, he's the fast gun with the crooked nose. Hop, he's the biggest and meanest, always in fights, nearly killed a man last week over cards. Beat him to a pulp."

"Nice fellows."

Paxton grunted, then shoved a cigar into his mouth. "Yeah."

"That's a cavalry holster you're wearing."

"That's a fact. Fought Apaches. I got shot up plenty and mustered out. Still have the miseries now and then."

"You knew Ethan Mandell in Arizona?"

"Nope. Big country down there. Heard of 'im, though. He mostly scouted. Never lost a trail, they say."

Tyler went outside. It was a warm, sunny day. He was hungry and he needed a bath, so he visited the local barber. He had to see Ethan again, but he wanted to be clean.

After a visit to the barber, he went to the general store, where he changed into a new blue shirt and britches. He pulled on his same black leather vest, the pockets indispensable, and then bought a new leather coat. Then he walked across the street and down to the jailhouse.

His thoughts were churning. He wanted to hang around Ethan, to learn more about him, to make up his own mind about the man. What better way than to be his deputy?

He stepped onto the boardwalk and proceeded to the jailhouse door. Swallowing, he opened the door and stepped inside. The jail was clean and neat with a stove in the back, next to the door that led to the cells. Bunks were at the left and right walls of the office. The only windows were the two up front on each side of the door.

Antlers of a big mule deer hung over the desk that faced the back wall to the right. Below the antlers was a big Sharps rifle, and on the other side of the desk was a gun rack, heavy with rifles, carbines, and shotguns.

Ethan sat at the desk shuffling papers. He held a cup of coffee in his left hand, and he turned and leaned back in his big wooden chair.

"Sit down, Tyler."

Pulling up a chair, Tyler took an offered cup of coffee and looked at the hot, thick liquid. Then he gazed at the lawman. Ethan was handsome, big, and well muscled. There was a lot of gray in the thick red-brown hair and the long mustache. His face was weathered and lined deep with a lot of history.

"I looked through all my handbills, Tyler, and you ain't in 'em. But I sure feel like I seen you before somewhere."

"We've never met."

"You thought about my offer? Thirty a month."

"I was making that much herding cows down near Socorro."

"Who'd you work for?"

"The River Bar spread. Man named Hawkens. Why?"

"Just wondered. You got any family?"

"Nope."

"Never been married?"

Tyler shrugged. "Nope."

His thoughts scrambled, Tyler wanted desperately to question Ethan about his past, but he fought the urge. Until he was brave enough to learn the truth about this man, he would keep on suffering.

Ethan's voice interrupted Tyler's thoughts: "This job includes that bunk over there and chuck at the hotel."

Tyler sipped his coffee with a frown. "Well, maybe if you let me make the coffee."

"Good. Let me swear you in right now."

They both stood up. As he took the oath to support the law and the Constitution, Tyler was stiff and short of breath. Then Ethan pinned the star on his leather vest with great difficulty. When they shook hands, Tyler came to the realization that his whole life was changing.

Ethan sat back down and wrote out a report of last night's shooting. Tyler signed it, then wrote his own report on how he found the body of Jody Rollins, with no signs of the killer. Ethan was impressed with the neat handwriting.

"You've had some schoolin', I see."

"When I was a boy, I wanted to be a lawyer and run for the Senate. But I quit school when I was fourteen."

"Too bad."

Tyler leaned back in the wooden chair and accepted another cup of coffee. "I woke up this morning with a gun in my face. Some fellow named Slap Dooley. I think he's a little crazy."

"I know about Slap. He acts weird, all right, but it's his three brothers you got to watch out for. Hop's the meanest and biggest. They say he once killed a man with his hands. Skip is the fast gun. Jump is the edgy one. Any one of 'em would shoot you in the back."

"I hear they work for Crocker."

"Yeah, they guard his freight."

"He said the man that tried to gun you was named Luke Smithers."

"So I found out." Ethan studied him a long moment. "Why did you quit school?"

"I ran off and joined the volunteers. Lied about my age, but I had a lot of company. Fought for the Union."

Tyler wanted to brag about how he won a commendation in battle, and to mention how he would lie terrified at night, staring at the stars and listening to the silence as he awaited the dawn and another bloody fight. He had a strange need to share his past with this man.

Ethan leaned forward, his elbow on his desk. "Now, that's interestin'. Glad you survived. Ain't many did. Me, I joined the Army all right, but they sent me off to fight Apaches. I mustered out in Arizona Territory after the war was over."

"You got a family?"

Ethan seemed to reel from the personal question, and he turned to his papers, his hand tight on a pencil. "No."

Tyler felt his face burning. He was so tense he couldn't move for a while. He worried that the only way he would ever learn if this man was his father was to ask him outright, and he didn't want to do that yet.

Ethan stood up and said, "I'm going to the funeral. You stay here."

"Thanks. I wasn't looking to tangle with Celia Rollins, not until she calms down."

"When I get back, we'll go over to the north side."

"You figure to find out who hired that fellow to gun you?"

"That ain't likely, but I got to show we ain't afraid."

Ethan left and Tyler sat down at the lawman's desk. He

27

studied the man's handwriting, and then looked through the handbills, getting familiar with the faces of men he might never see.

He opened the drawers and saw a mess of papers. Ethan sure wasn't very neat. He closed the drawers and stood up and paced around. He went into the back room and saw the two cells, both empty, with a heavily barred back door between them. The only windows were small ones above each enclosure.

After a time he sat down at the desk, put his feet up, and enjoyed a cup of his own coffee, which tasted a lot better than Ethan's. He even slept awhile.

Later, he was startled by the door swinging open. Putting his feet down, he turned to see Celia standing there in a dark dress and shawl. There was black lace over her yellow hair. She marched inside, leaving the door open. He stumbled to his feet, knowing that behind her pretty face with its hot anger were heartache and unresolved grief.

"I came to say I'm sorry," she said. "But I still think you could have killed my brother. That badge don't mean nothin'."

Tyler pushed his hat back from his forehead. "I sure like the way you apologize."

Celia folded her arms, trying to stand taller. "Then prove you didn't do it. Go right over and arrest Crocker."

"I'll do this much—I'll go over and talk to him. But as soon as you're able, I'd like you to show me the road you take to the pass, and where some of the accidents occurred."

"What good will that do?"

"Look, Miss Celia, I can't help you if you don't trust me."

"I don't know anything about you."

"For the last ten years, I've been herding cattle down in Texas and New Mexico Territory."

"And before that?"

"I worked on the Mississippi."

"A gambler?"

"No, I worked for freighters. Maybe three years."

"And before that?"

He frowned as his temper rose. "I was in the war."

"You were a boy."

"That's right."

Her pretty face twisted slightly. "Which side?"

"The Union."

"Wrong side."

"Do you want help or not?"

Celia glared at him, her gaze fixed on his perplexed but patient expression. And then she flushed. He walked over to her as she straightened.

"All right, Mr. Sinclair. I still think you killed my brother, but I can't prove it. So let's call a truce." He gazed down at her for a long while. He decided that her eyes were blue with green flecks. She sure was lovely to look at when her face was washed. But so was a cougar.

"I still don't know why you're here, Mr. Sinclair." She looked him over, her gaze fixed a moment on his low-slung holster and the well-oiled Colt. Then she turned, just as Ethan came up the boardwalk and joined her in the doorway.

The lawman tipped his hat. "Everything all right, Miss Celia?"

"I was just apologizing to Mr. Sinclair."

Tyler hooked his thumbs in his gun belt. "Sort of." She tossed her head, turned away, and strutted down the street.

Tyler watched her until she passed out of sight.

Ethan looked at Tyler with curiosity. "You got something goin' on there?"

Tyler shrugged. "Not likely."

"Well, let's head on over and see Crocker."

As the two men walked along the boardwalk toward the bridge, Tyler kept glancing at the lawman. They were both tall and had big shoulders and lean bodies. Ethan's stride was catlike, smooth and easy, but he often limped a little, favoring his left leg. His large hands rested loose and ready at his sides.

"How'd you hurt your leg?" Tyler asked.

Ethan grimaced. "Got that in Tucson. Fellow named Ratner."

"What happened?"

"Got 'im between the eyes."

"I read about that. He had two men with him, and you got all three."

"Guess I was lucky."

The stage was coming up the river. The driver and guard waved, and Ethan waved back. On the top, along with the luggage, were several rough-looking men.

"Miners," Ethan said. "They rent horses from Filer to get to the mines. The freighters bring 'em back."

Ethan was first onto the bridge, and Tyler turned to peer back at the street. Sweetwater looked like a lot of frontier towns, the main street lined with shops and saloons and other establishments, and its houses spread out all around.

Looking north, he saw the typical bad side of any town—a busy street lined with horses, saloons, dance halls, and gaming rooms. He followed Ethan across the bridge, which was about six feet wide, with a railing, and about thirty feet across to the other side of the deep, roaring water.

"Miner dumped a load of sugar in it once," Ethan said. "That's how it got its name. It's some ten-feet deep along here and ice cold, and anybody falls in, you almost never find 'im in time. Our old bridge got washed out last winter, but this one's higher and holdin' on so far."

Tyler matched stride with the man, and soon they were on another boardwalk on the east side of the street, walking by saloons that were already filled with miners and drifters. Only a few merchants seemed involved at the tables. He saw no women in the gaming saloons, but when they passed the dance hall, he saw several inside the swinging doors. They looked drab and weary.

On the left was Crocker's express office. Just past it, a gunsmith was doing a land-office business.

Farther up on the right was the Crocker freight office, with several horses at the hitching rail. Just beyond the office was a large, deep, watering trough next to a long-handled pump. Behind it were corrals, wagons, horses and mules, and a lot of flies.

On the bench in front of the express office was a seedy character of great size, wearing baggy pants, a dirty shirt stretched over his fat belly, and a well-oiled six-gun at his side. His hat was perched back on a heap of curly brown hair, and his dark eyes were fixed on the lawmen. He had a fat face and a small, round mouth.

"Well, if it ain't the law," he sneered.

Ethan paused and looked at him with disinterest. "Don't you ever work, Hop?"

"Hey, the Dooleys do more work around here than anybody. And what's it to you, *Marshal*? With that nose, you oughta be up at the mines, diggin' ditches."

The man laughed like a hyena. Ethan ignored him and entered the office, but Tyler paused on the boardwalk, irritation coloring his hot face. So this was one of Slap's brothers. Hop was the one who had killed a man with his hands. Also, he had a nasty mouth, and Tyler didn't like it.

"What are you lookin' at, Deputy?"

"I ain't sure. You smell like a skunk, look like a toad, and wear your clothes like you found them in some alley."

Tyler would never know why he challenged the man. Maybe it was the sinister defiance, or the condescending attitude. Or it could be that he just needed some exercise. And just maybe, it was because the man had insulted Ethan.

But Tyler was soon to regret his insult.

Hop Dooley roared off his seat and landed in the middle of Tyler like a mad grizzly. He knocked the wind from him, and they went crashing into the street. Next, two hundred and fifty pounds slammed onto Tyler's chest.

They rolled up against the watering trough. Then Tyler broke free. But he was grabbed again, and they rolled back into the open near the horses at the railing.

Dazed, the world spinning, Tyler twisted his head from under the big hand. He smelled the man's dirty sweat and felt the great weight as he struggled to get out from under it. Dust flew so thick around them that it choked him.

"I'm gonna kill you!" Hop snarled.

Tyler squirmed free, rose to one knee, and slammed his right fist deep in Hop's fat gut. As Hop gasped, he next hit Hop's hard jaw, nearly breaking his left hand, and drawing back with a silent gasp as his fingers stung.

Hop got to his knees, his big face puffed, and his eyes round and bulging as he fought for breath. A crowd was gathering. Someone was placing bets on how long Tyler would live.

Tyler staggered to his feet. He was out of breath and shaken from Hop's crushing weight, and his body ached with pain. Now they stalked each other like roosters, Hop's giant hands held out like hungry jaws.

"Come on," Hop snickered.

Sweat covering his entire body, Tyler could feel his mouth gone so dry that it hurt. He had to stay out of reach of those hands. He couldn't run away, but he could end up mashed into the dirt. Heart beating like crazy, he moistened his lips and rubbed his sore hands.

Now Tyler began to dance a little, moving his fists around. His new Stetson was on the ground near a horse's hoof. He had to keep fighting or lose face—or even his life.

Suddenly Hop rushed him. But Tyler sidestepped and Hop went sprawling into a nearby horse and then between its legs. The animal kicked and bucked frantically as the crowd laughed. Hop got free and struggled to his feet. As he turned, his face beet-red, the laughter stopped.

Hop charged again, and this time, he seized Tyler by the right arm and lifted him like a toy. Tyler slammed his knee into the man's gut. Hop gasped, but he threw Tyler down and pounced on him with a fury.

Tyler rolled free as Hop hit the dirt. He jumped up and kicked Hop in the rear, nearly breaking his foot. Hop got up with a roar, and turned and rushed at Tyler.

They grappled, hit the dirt, and rolled under the dancing hooves of another horse, whose iron shoes kept stamping near their heads.

They rolled clear to the other side near the trough, the crowd following and circling. Hop was winded, but his huge hands were like vises on Tyler's arms.

As they staggered to their feet, Tyler suddenly swept up his fists, broke free, and backed away. He knew he couldn't take another hit from this bear of a man. They stalked each other again. Tyler backed up near the trough, so tired he could hardly stand.

Suddenly Hop charged with an animal roar. When Tyler jumped aside, Hop tried to stop his rush, but he lost his balance and tumbled into the trough on his belly. He fought to get up, but Tyler leaped on his back, grabbed him around the neck, and tried to keep him down.

Hop came up with a roar and spun around to face Tyler. Hop threw Tyler with ease, but then Hop lost his balance and sat down backward in the trough with his feet rising straight up in the air.

Hop was stuck. His rear end was down deep and squeezed tight between the sides of the trough, and water was up to his armpits. He roared like a lion and tried to pull himself up. He couldn't move anything but his arms and feet, and he looked ridiculous.

The crowd fought back their laughter, all afraid of Hop.

Tyler stood fighting for breath. He was in no hurry to continue the fight. He hurt all over and his gut was churning. He moved back as two men, who looked like mule skinners in their rough clothing and beards, came forward and tried to pull Hop out of the trough. But Hop was stuck, no matter what his friends did. They tried to turn him sideways and struggled to lift him. Finally they stood back in frustration.

Tyler recovered his Stetson, smashed several times, and tried to reshape it. Then he looked up to see Ethan standing on the boardwalk, looking curious and amused. Next to him, looking disgusted, was a big man with blond hair and a huge jaw, a pipe between his teeth.

"Don't you break my trough," the blond man warned the rescuers.

One of the men looked up from Hop's side. "We can't get him out, Mr. Crocker. We got to break it."

"Don't you dare break that trough! I'm mighty proud of it, seein' as how it was here long before this town ever was."

"Ain't no other way," one of the men said.

Crocker folded his arms. "Take somethin' and pry him up."

The crowd grew larger as the two men brought iron bars and wooden blocks from the toolshed behind the office. After hooking the bars under Hop's arms and over the blocks, they put all their weight down as Hop shoved at the trough's sides.

Tyler pulled on his hat as he stepped onto the boardwalk.

"Hop's really going to be mad," Ethan said.

Crocker grunted. "He'll be too cold to do anything now. That water was nearly frozen this mornin'."

They heard a cheer from the crowd as Hop rose from the water, legs and arms swinging. His friends grabbed him as he fell forward. He began yelling about his back.

"I'm broke! I'm broke in two!"

"You'll be all right," one of his friends assured him.

But Hop could barely straighten, and two of them took him

by the arm and helped him across the street toward a seedy hotel. Some of the crowd followed while others drifted away, the show over.

"Now then," Crocker said. "You wanted to see me, Marshal? Come back inside and have a drink."

Tyler and Ethan followed him inside. Crocker sat down behind his huge walnut desk and shoved a bottle and glasses toward them. The office was rather ornate for the north side of town. Paintings of cowboys on the range were all over the walls. The head of a buffalo hung over two Sharps rifles behind him.

"Help yourself," Crocker said, stoking his pipe.

"No, thanks," Ethan said. He sat down stiffly in one of the wooden chairs while Tyler sat wearily on a bench near the door with his back to the wall.

Crocker leaned back. "How about your deputy there? He looks in terrible shape."

Tyler knew he looked as crunched up as tobacco in a sack, but he tried to appear aloof by hooking his sore thumbs in his gun belt. He was hurting, but he had no taste for whiskey.

"No, thanks," he responded.

Ethan looked straight at Crocker as he said, "Fellow named Luke Smithers tried to bushwhack me last night. Tyler here shot him afore he could get me in the back. He's buried out on boot hill."

Crocker frowned. "Sorry to hear that. Luke never was the same after they tried to hang 'im down in Pueblo for shootin' a feller. He was kickin' up there half the night, and finally they cut 'im down. The town just figured he had to be innocent since he was still alive. Of course, he was guilty as sin. But folks around here kind of admired Luke."

"He work for you?" Ethan asked.

Crocker poured himself a drink and licked the glass. "No, he didn't. He always seemed to have money, though. Must have worked for somebody."

Ethan pushed his hat back. "Another thing. Tyler here found Jody Rollins out in the valley yesterday, shot in the back."

"I heard about that. But I can't help you there, either."

"You had good reason to get rid of ole man Rollins and his son," Ethan said. "You were here first, and they've been cutting into your business."

"Marshal, I'm a fair man and welcome competition. Besides, them little wagons can't haul half my loads."

"But your big wagons hardly make it up to the camps."

Crocker sipped his whiskey. "Don't mean nothin'."

Tyler was getting sick to his stomach. He still felt Hop's fist in his middle, and his left hand still cringed from hitting Hop's hard jaw.

Ethan stood up. "Where are the other Dooleys?"

"Slap and Jump, they're guardin' a shipment," Crocker said. "Skip went to Denver for me on business."

Ethan went outside, and a weary Tyler followed him. The sun was already low over the western mountains, and a chill was setting in as twilight drew near. Tyler could hardly walk as he tried to keep pace with Ethan. The lawman walked down the middle of the dusty street, heading back toward the bridge.

On the wooden planks, Ethan stopped, then turned to look at Tyler's crippled gait. He grinned. "You all right, son?"

"Yeah, but that big ox nearly killed me."

The sun disappeared in a glow of red and yellow. The distant mountains looked dark and cold while the surrounding foothills were still green and bright.

Ethan was still studying Tyler. "What made you lay into him, anyhow?"

"Didn't like his looks."

"Or what he said about me?"

Tyler knew he was reddening. "When I ride for the brand, I don't want no one making smart remarks."

Ethan grinned. "Is that a fact?"

"Besides, he was asking for it."

"Even if he was twice your size."

"He didn't look that big sittin' down."

"Especially in the water trough."

Tyler started walking again. "Yeah."

"He'll be madder than a woke-up grizzly."

The two men walked side by side, with Ethan casting glances at Tyler, who sensed admiration and respect. The feeling was so welcome, he didn't know what to do about it.

"I'll buy you supper," Ethan said.

"No, thanks. I got to lie down."

"Then I'll bring you some. Sure you're all right?"

"I will be."

Ethan left, and Tyler went alone into the jailhouse. He could barely move his arms to light the lamps, and when he hit his bunk in the corner, he hurt so bad it kept him awake for at least two minutes.

* * *

While Tyler slept, Ethan had his meal at the hotel, ordered

a meal in a box for Tyler, then stopped at the freight office. Maggie was working on the books while Celia soaped her saddle. Ethan removed his hat. As usual, he felt awkward around Maggie. Both women had obviously been crying. He swallowed hard before speaking: "Just wanted to see if you two were all right." Then he told them about Tyler's fight with Hop. Maggie frowned. "Was Tyler hurt bad?"

"Sort of. But Tyler won, if you can call it that. Hop ended up sittin' in Crocker's waterin' trough, and he got stuck. They had to pry him out."

"Good," Maggie said with a weak smile.

Celia looked from Maggie to Ethan, and seeing the shy glances between them, she suddenly stood up and made an excuse to go into the back room.

Ethan was embarrassed to be alone with Maggie, and he started to leave, but she stood up and walked around the desk.

"Ethan, can I talk to you a minute?"

"Sure, Maggie."

"I'm worried about this Tyler Sinclair and what Celia's been saying. We don't know much about him. Do you?"

"No, but I sent word by stage to Socorro, about the ranch where he was workin'. Maybe I'll hear back in a week or so. But I'll tell you this much—what I do know, I like."

Maggie touched his arm with her soft white hand. "Thank you, Ethan. You're a good friend."

He flushed with color. "Well, uh, I got to be goin'."

She sat down behind her desk and grasped some of the papers. "I just ordered another Studebaker wagon," she said. "Cost me a hundred and forty this time. And ten for the wagon cover. But I ain't sure I want to spend twenty dollars on a spring seat."

"You and Celia are doin' yourself proud."

"Well, I buried my husband a long time back, and now I had to bury Jody. But Celia sure tries to take their place. I'm real scared she's gonna get hurt, Ethan. You tell that Tyler to mind his manners and to look out for her, will you?"

"I won't have to." He turned and walked to the door, then paused to look back at her. She was gazing at him with such softness that he hurried outside.

Maggie got up to bar the door, and Celia came into the room. "I heard, Mama."

"I swear, that's the most hard-to-get man I ever saw. Percy Filer follows me around like a puppy dog, and Ethan runs away."

"He's carryin' a lot of misery."

"I wish I knew what it was," Maggie said. "We've had a long day. Let's get some rest."

"I'm worried. If Tyler Sinclair is a hired gun, then Ethan isn't safe."

"But Tyler saved the marshal's life."

"It could have been to get in good with him."

"So you don't like Tyler?"

Celia frowned. "Not after I saw him standing over Jody and no one else around for miles."

"Well, I like the young man. Let's hope you're wrong about him."

Celia nodded, but her thoughts were confused. She was attracted to Tyler, and she hated it because she was still certain he had killed her brother.

* * *

40

Ethan walked back up the street toward the jailhouse. He paused to check some of the doors on the dark shops. He was still shaken by Maggie's nearness.

He tried to think of something else, like his new deputy who seemed to be here for some secret endeavor. He was certain he had met the young man before.

Ethan crossed the street toward the jail where Tyler was sleeping, and then he stopped. He could see over on the north side in the moonlight, and there was something going on near the freight office. A lot of men were standing around a wagon.

Checking his six-gun to be sure it was loose in his holster, he walked to the bridge and across the empty street of the north side. The night was silent and he could still see the men by the wagon, but there was no sound of voices, no movement. Until the crack of a rifle shattered the stillness.

THREE

The rifle bullet struck Ethan across the back, cutting his left shoulder area, knocking him forward and down to his knees. Six-gun in hand, he tried to fight the shock and brutal blow of the bullet. His back was numb, his left arm frozen, and his heart beat fast.

He rose on one knee, fighting to stay conscious. He had to get to the boardwalk, to shelter. As he started to rise, another bullet struck him a few inches below the back of his left shoulder. He spun and dropped down, trying to see where the bullet had come from. But he was unable to get back up. He lay on his right side, hurting now, and scanning the roof tops and alleys with blurred vision.

He heard running feet on the bridge south of him.

Trying to rise on his elbow, he saw Tyler hurrying toward him, shirtless, and with Paxton at his heels. Tyler reached him and dropped to his side.

"You all right, Ethan?"

"I'm fadin' fast."

Paxton knelt beside them. "I don't see nothin'."

"Came from the left over there, the west side," Ethan muttered.

Tyler looked around at the dark, empty street and felt the silence. There was no safety here, no shelter. "We'll get you back across. Then I'll look around."

"No. He's gone by now. Ain't worth it. They'd just be waitin' for you."

The two men lifted Ethan and, making a chair of their arms, carried him quickly back toward the bridge. Their hearts were pounding; at any moment they could all be cut down.

"The wagon still there?" Ethan murmured.

"No wagon. Nobody in the street," Tyler said. They carried Ethan across the bridge, breathing easier now. They took him into the jail and let him lie on his bunk on his right side, his back to the wall. He was bleeding badly. Paxton went for the doctor and Tyler set about cutting off Ethan's shirt.

The lawman's eyes were closing, and his voice was weak: "You took a big chance comin' after me. You and Paxton."

"They can't get away with this."

"We got no proof, son."

"I'll go back over there."

"No, and that's an order."

And with that, Ethan was unconscious. Tyler felt his eyes stinging, and he bit his lip. Peeling the lawman's torn shirt from the wounds in his back, he realized he was holding his breath. He turned the man a little more on his stomach and began to wash the blood away with a towel. This man was too brave to be his father.

After a few minutes, Paxton and the wiry doctor, who had pulled his britches over his underwear, came inside. With help, the doctor dug out the bullets, which were close to the surface, from the unconscious lawman's back. Tyler pulled on a shirt and tried to help. The doctor finally finished.

"He'll be all right if there ain't no infection. They weren't all that deep. You keep an eye on him. Some fever might be expected, but if he gets to sweating bad, you call me."

When the doctor was gone, Tyler covered Ethan with blankets, then sat down at the desk and wiped his face with his bandanna. Paxton pulled up a chair.

"Tyler, that's a tough old man."

"I oughta go back over there and have a look."

"Ethan's right. As soon as you and me showed, whoever done it took off. Won't do no good now, and you'll just run into an ambush."

*   *   *

From then on, it was up to Tyler to keep an eye on things. Maggie came the next day, frantic. Celia brought food. Tyler and Paxton strolled the north side several times, but everyone looked innocent.

For a few days Ethan was in weak condition, but then he became more alert and could sit up on his own. Tyler was relieved, but he kept a close watch on the man. He often played his harmonica, which Ethan seemed to enjoy.

When the mail was brought one afternoon, Ethan was able to sit at his desk and sort through it on his own, though his left arm was in a sling. He opened one letter and read it in silence. After a moment, he looked at Tyler, who was standing nearby.

"Well, son, I got a letter from Mr. Hawkens at the Bar River spread."

"You wrote him?"

"Was checkin' on you. Wanta read it?"

Tyler grinned. "Don't matter. I know just what he said. 'That Tyler wasn't good for nothing.' "

Ethan read it aloud: " 'Dear Marshal Mandell, I got your letter and I was glad to know Tyler is working for you. It'll do him good, as I always figured he would rather sit around the campfire and sing and play that fool mouth harp than work cattle.

" 'But I got to tell you, in a stampede or a fight there ain't nobody I'd rather have on my side. I don't know much about him before he come here, but he was an honest young fellow. He was here about three years and he rode for the brand. I'd hire him back any day. Your friend, Jake Hawkens.' "

Ethan folded the letter and handed it to Tyler, who, with some embarrassment, took it and slid it into his vest pocket.

"I liked that old man," Tyler said.

"I reckon you know I had to check on you some, because you're wearin' a Federal badge and all."

"Don't matter. I expected it."

"Still doesn't tell me why you came to Sweetwater."

"I already said I was lookin' for a change."

Ethan studied him awhile, then continued, "Celia Rollins was here this afternoon. She's ready to show you where the wagons were hit. I've been there, but maybe you'll see somethin' I didn't."

"Seems like if the Dooleys had done the wagon damage, even with masks, they'd have been recognized."

Ethan accepted a cup of coffee. "The men drivin' the wagons, and half the town, are plenty scared of the Dooleys, and sure wouldn't tell on 'em."

There was a knock at the door. Tyler opened it to find Celia standing there. She was wearing a green dress, and her hair was tied back. She handed him a bottle of what looked like potato soup. There was still a lot of hostility in her glance, but she sure looked pretty.

Tyler stared a moment, then flushed. "Uh, Miss Celia, I was wondering when you wanted to show me where the trouble was."

"Tomorrow at sunup. I'll be outside our office."

"You gonna bring a picnic lunch?"

She was surprised and visibly annoyed. "Why should I?"

"Because I'm the law."

Celia stared at his serious frown, and then, despite herself, she laughed. It was the prettiest, most musical laugh he had ever heard, and he smiled. But she quickly recovered and frowned at him, her nose in the air.

"Well, I suppose we do have to eat."

Ethan was grinning. "Maybe he'll play his harmonica."

Tyler was uneasy. "I don't play it much anymore."

"Bring it along," Celia said.

Then she turned and walked out into the sunlight, pausing to glance back at him. Tyler closed the door and felt his face burning. He had no urge to play his music in front of a woman. Maybe he would leave his harmonica behind accidentally.

"I wish you hadn't told her," Tyler said to Ethan.

Ethan was still grinning like a fool. "You play right well. Maybe it'll win her over. She still doesn't trust you."

"I ain't never played in front of a woman."

"It might rain," Ethan warned. "You watch out for sudden floods up there. That trail gets mighty slippery, and it's plenty narrow in spots, hardly wide enough for the Crocker wagons. Goes right along a cliff in some parts."

"Will you be all right if I'm gone for the day?"

"You already been fussin' over me like a mother hen, but go ahead and get Paxton to stay over here tomorrow if you'll feel better about it."

"I'll do that."

"Anyhow, he makes a whole lot better coffee than you."

Tyler built up the fire in the iron stove. Then he shared the delicious soup with Ethan. After a time, Ethan lay back and closed his eyes.

"Play that there mouth harp for me, son."

Tyler sat on his bunk, a bit uneasy, but he drew it out and tapped it on his knee a little. Then he lay on the bunk and began to play "I Ride an Old Paint." Unexpectedly, Ethan began to sing in a deep voice:

> " '*Oh, when I die, take my saddle from the wall,*
> *Put it on my pony, lead him out of his stall,*
> *Tie my bones to his back, turn our faces to the west,*
> *And we'll ride the prairies that we love the best.*' "

Tyler couldn't look at the lawman. He kept his gaze on his boots as he lounged on the bunk. The more songs he played, the more Ethan sang in a good, deep voice, carrying the tune with a lot of heart. Tyler couldn't help but enjoy the sharing.

Soon, there was no singing. Tyler kept playing, but when

he turned his head, Ethan was sound asleep. And so he, too, turned in for the night.

*   *   *

At the crack of dawn, Tyler washed his face and gathered a tarp, slicker, and some gear. Then he trekked over to the livery, saddled his black horse, and slid his Winchester into the scabbard. He wore his new leather coat over his shirt and vest.

When he rode down toward the Rollins freight office, he realized he was looking forward to riding with Celia, even though she was still wondering if he might have killed her brother. It wasn't quite daylight when he saw her.

She was astride a bay mare, with a covered basket fastened to the pommel of her saddle. She, too, had a slicker behind the cantle, but she looked bright-eyed and ready to go in her buckskin jacket and riding skirt. Her face was rosy, and her hair was tied back under her man's hat with the chin strap pulled tight. Under her jacket was a gun belt and small revolver.

"Did you bring your harmonica?"

"Maybe I did, maybe I didn't."

She turned her bay mare toward the creek. Tyler rode alongside her. The sky was mostly clouds. Dark ones moved swiftly to the east, where streaks of red hung on the horizon. The wind was rising and there was a chill. Celia led the way to the bridge, then turned without crossing and headed for the western mountains along a well-traveled wagon road on the south side of the rushing water.

They spent half the morning crossing a lot of valley floor with the mountains ever beckoning. Then they began to climb gradually. They rode in silence, enjoying the cold wind, the sweet smell of green grass, the scattered yellow flowers, and the emptiness all around them. Trees began to appear along the creek, some willows and cottonwoods, and then brilliant aspens with shimmering emerald leaves. Pines covered the ridges. All in all, it wasn't a bad way to spend a day.

*   *   *

But while Tyler and Celia were enjoying themselves, Wiley Crocker was storming about his office. Jump Dooley stood near the door, his big body and face taut at the fury in Crocker's voice. Jump's beard dripped with tobacco juice.

Slap was sitting on a chair, legs crossed, smirking, his dark eyes shadowed by heavy lids.

"Listen to me, boys!" Crocker roared. "I ain't losin' no more wagons!"

"But it just plumb turned over, boss," Jump said. "I was up ahead on the trail, but when I turned around, the wagon was just slidin' off the cliff. The boys got off just in time, and they got the mules free."

"All that mining equipment cost me a lot of money!"

Jump swallowed, then wet his lips. "Boss, it just proves that them wagons are too big and wide for that pass. You need some like Rollins got."

"I ain't givin' 'em the satisfaction. And I aim to make sure they lose a wagon now and then, just enough to worry 'em. Sooner or later, we'll put 'em out of business."

"Ain't worked yet," Jump said.

"We'll finish 'em when I'm ready."

"That Miss Celia—I saw her ridin' out this mornin' with that Tyler Sinclair. Headin' for the pass. Looked like they was goin' on a picnic."

Crocker sneered. "Good. Go make sure he don't come back."

Slap snickered and then chuckled. "Ole Hop, he'd like to do it hisself. He couldn't straighten up all night after he got stuck in that trough."

"Hop's still up at the mine," Crocker said. "You boys take care of it now. And don't leave no witnesses."

"I ain't killin' no woman," Jump declared.

"What about you, Slap?"

"You'd have to pay plenty."

Crocker grunted. "You'll be well paid. But you may not have to kill her if she don't see you. I'll let you figure it out. But we got to get rid of them lawmen or we'll never get our town back."

Jump grunted. "I'd've got the marshal if he hadn't turned suddenly. But I did put two bullets in 'im."

"We'll get the job done," Slap said with assurance. "But it ain't gonna be easy. I wish Skip was here."

Crocker looked at the clock on the wall. "When Skip gets back from Denver, we may be needin' his fast gun if you don't take care of things. But right now, it's up to you boys. Get up there and get it done! I don't wanta see Tyler Sinclair anymore—unless he's dead!"

FOUR

By early afternoon, Tyler and Celia had reached the pass. They rode single file with Tyler in the lead. The sky was dark and gloomy, but the air was crisp and the green of the land was a delight. Pines caressed the ridges above, and far below on their right, the creek sang with white water as it raced deep and wild between its rocky walls. The hills rose so high around them that they couldn't see the snow-crested mountains.

Celia had already pointed out two places where her wagons had been dumped from the high banks into the creek, and they had also seen one of Crocker's down in the rocks. Now the trail was steep and barely wide enough for a wagon, with the water some fifty feet below on their right. They were getting mighty hungry.

"Over there," she said, pointing to a rise on their left. In the clearing against the granite walls, lush grass awaited them beneath a stately aspen, its leaves murmuring in the wind.

They tethered their horses and loosened the cinches. Then Tyler spread his tarp under the tree. She sat opposite him and opened the basket. After peeling away the cloth, she brought out a bottle of cider, cookies, and fried chicken.

"Where did you get chicken?"

She smiled with pride. "Mules aren't all we have in our back corrals, Mr. Sinclair. We have chickens and plenty of eggs."

"Must make you mighty popular."

"But in the winter we have to keep the hens inside. My mother's a terrific cook, you know. We've had the marshal over for supper a couple of times, but he sure is afraid of her, not like that Percy Filer who keeps hanging around."

"Filer, the banker?"

"Yes, and his son, Peter. They've been good to us, making loans to keep us going. But they've also lent a lot of money to Crocker. If times got bad, Filer would foreclose on the two freight lines."

"You bad in debt?"

"If we lose any more wagons, we're done for. Since the marshal came, though, the wagons are getting through."

Tyler tasted the chicken, and it was delicious. When they had finished eating, there was still a lot of chicken and cookies left. Tyler was so satisfied that, his hands behind his head, he laid back, ready to sleep.

"Mr. Sinclair, I didn't bring you up here to nap. I want to hear some music."

He gazed at her from under his hat brim. "I didn't bring my harmonica."

"Then what's that stickin' out of your vest pocket?"

He flushed and drew out the instrument. Maybe, if he wasn't looking at her, it would be all right. But it sure was mighty pleasant to be here on a hilltop and right next to a real pretty woman, even if she was suspicious and difficult.

As he played his music, he felt warm suddenly as she started to sing in a clear, sweet voice that gave him the shivers.

Tyler's heart was swelling in his chest. He played more ballads, and she seemed to know them all, even the "Zebra Dun." They were songs that were sung nights around the cattle to keep them quiet, and songs a man would sing when alone. He closed his eyes as he played, enjoying her voice. When he rested at last, he peered at her from under his hat.

"How did you learn all these songs?"

"I lived most of my life in Texas on a ranch, but we left when the carpetbaggers came. My father sold everything and bought this freight contract right out from under Percy Filer's nose as soon as we hit town. The former owner couldn't handle Crocker and wanted to quit."

"Are you and your ma gonna keep at it?"

"It's all we have, Mr. Sinclair."

"You could get killed."

"Not with two Federal marshals in town."

He grunted and began to play more of his music. But the sky was darkening, and soon it started to rain. They jumped up and gathered her things into the tarp. "Up there," she said, "under that rock."

They ran across the deep grass with rain hitting them at full force. She went ahead of him, climbing the grade toward the boulders, but she suddenly slipped and fell face-down into the wet grass. The rain was so heavy that they could hardly see. She slid some more as Tyler knelt at her side.

With the tarp gathered in his right hand, he grabbed her right arm with his left and pulled her to her feet.

She slid some more, falling against him and grabbing at his arms. She barely came to his chin as she held on and then looked up. The heavy downpour was bending her hat brim down around her face.

Her hands were on his arms above the elbow as she held on and slipped some more. Rain poured off their hats and coats. His left arm went around her waist as she kept staring up at him. She was pretty and pink and breathless, and Tyler couldn't help himself.

He bent his knees and lowered his head, his lips suddenly catching and holding hers in a long, sweet kiss that sent wild sensations through him. She tasted as delicious as cider. When he drew back, they were both out of breath, and she was still staring at him. His face was red-hot.

She tried to move away from him, but her boots skidded again on the grade, and he turned with her, keeping his arm about her waist and helping her up the grade to the shelter. In the slim protection of the overhanging rocks, she slid from his arm and sank down to the narrow spot of dry earth. The cover was less than they had thought.

Tyler leaned back on the granite and stared at the deluge. Kissing her had not been in his plans. He was mighty attracted to her, as any man would be, but he couldn't let himself be vulnerable to a woman. And it was obvious that Celia was pretty upset over his attention.

"We have to find shelter," she said. "We can't stay here."

"That trail up was pretty steep. Ain't safe."

"There's a cabin farther on."

Suddenly, thunder boomed in the dark rolls of the clouds, and then lightning began to spit across the sky. Celia looked frightened, and her hair and skirts were soaked through, as was her waist under her jacket.

"How far up?" Tyler asked, worried about her.

"A mile, I think. We use it for wagon stops."

"We got to get down to the horses. But you wait here until I get your slicker."

"No, I'll go with you."

Before they could move, lightning struck the aspen where they had been picnicking. The trunk split open, and the great tree slanted but didn't fall. Celia shuddered, and her face had no color now. The horses had leaped sideways, sliding some.

Tyler took her cold hand and they started down the grade toward the nervous animals. She fell twice, but he pulled her to her feet. Reaching their mounts, they untied and drew on their yellow slickers. Then they tightened the cinches as the rain beat on them.

Tyler grabbed her arm to help her mount her bay mare, and then he swung astride his black. He tied the tarp filled with leftover food onto his pommel, and then they headed up the steep, narrow trail, with Tyler in the lead.

He glanced back often to be sure her mare was staying on the trail. The drop to the right, fifty feet down to the rocky and raging creek, was dangerous, and there was hardly any edge to the road. Rain was so heavy that the path ahead was barely visible.

They reached the rise as thunder rolled and lightning struck the treetops to the far right. Over against a cliff side to their left was a cabin in a grove of aspen. Smoke was curling from the chimney, but there were no horses or wagon in sight. Water was swirling around the structure.

They rode over and dismounted, and then loosened the cinches and tied their mounts to the railing. Tyler pulled his Winchester from the scabbard. Then they rushed to the steps and Tyler jerked the door open, the tarp full of food in one hand, his rifle in the other.

He led the way inside, then pulled the door shut behind them. It was a big cabin with one room, a stone hearth with a blazing fire, and a lot of wagon gear hanging from the wall and thrown about the floor. There were three cots on each side of the room and four chairs with a small table. A stack of dry wood rose nearly two feet high and several feet long against the back wall.

There were cans of beans and coffee on a shelf, cups and bowls next to them, and in the corner was a big, covered barrel of water. Pots, pans, and an old iron coffeepot were on the floor near the hearth.

And sitting on one of the bunks by the right wall was a boy of about ten, wearing a worn wool coat and denim pants. He had a round, freckled face and wide brown eyes. He was hugging a little black pup in his arms, and its pale eyes watched them as its lips curled back from its teeth.

"Hello," Celia said, hurrying to the fireside.

Tyler joined her and helped her take off her slicker and coat. She was drenched and chilled and trembling. They removed their dripping hats and hung them on hooks. Rain was drumming on the roof, and thunder was rolling in the sky. The rising wind shook the walls and rattled the front windows.

The boy watched them in silence. Tyler removed his slicker and coat, then went to one of the cots by the other wall and removed the blankets and carried them over to Celia.

"I'll hold one up while you get undressed. Then wrap yourself in another."

Shivering, she stared up at him, then glanced at the boy. Having company made her braver, and she nodded and rose to her feet. Tyler gave her two blankets, then took the other in both hands and held it across his back, arms outstretched to make a wall behind him. He faced the frightened boy, allowing her privacy.

"I'm Tyler Sinclair. And this is Celia Rollins."

"You come to arrest me?"

Tyler glanced down at the star on his vest. "Is there any reason I should?"

"I ain't done nothin'."

"Then you have nothing to worry about."

The boy hugged his dog. Tyler's arms were getting weary holding the blanket behind him. Finally Celia said, "All right."

He turned to see her wrapped in the two blankets right up to her chin, her gun belt in her hand. He went to the wagon gear and pulled down a set of reins, then walked over to her and slid one around her waist, tying it in front of her to keep the blankets warm about her.

All the while, she stared at his hands and then at his face. When she was belted in, she hung her waistcoat, underclothing, and skirt across a chair and moved it in front of the hearth. Next, she hung her gun belt on a wall hook.

Finally, still shivering, she sat down near the blazing fire. She folded her arms in her chill, but she seemed more concerned about the boy.

"What's your name?" she asked.

"Billy. And that's all I'm sayin'."

"You hungry, Billy?" Tyler asked.

"No."

Tyler put the tarp on the table and spread it out to reveal the leftover cider, chicken, and cookies. Billy's eyes got large and round, and Tyler beckoned. The boy hurried over, pulled up a chair, and began to help himself. He broke off pieces of meat to give to his dog.

"There's cans here," the boy said, his mouth full, "but I couldn't get 'em open."

"Did you come down from the mines?" Celia asked.

"Yeah, but I ain't goin' back."

"Where's your family?"

"I ain't got nothin' to say."

"Did you run away from home?" she asked.

The boy was silent and ate hungrily. Tyler found coffee on the shelf and filled a blackened pot with water from a barrel. The rain was fierce on the roof, and the wind was rattling the whole cabin. Thunder still rumbled in the sky, so low and loud that they thought the roof would cave in.

Tyler hung the pot over the fire, then sat opposite Billy and helped himself to a cookie. "I ran off when I was fourteen, but you can't be more than ten."

"You ran away from home?"

"Yep."

"Did they send you to an orphanage?"

"Nope. And I don't figure you'd have to worry about that. A lot of folks in town would sure take in a boy like you."

"You won't arrest me?"

"Nope."

"What if I ain't got no folks at all?"

Tyler swallowed, then ran his hand over his wet hair. "Then somebody would adopt you."

"No orphanage?"

"We ain't got one."

The boy looked relieved. "When my pa died up there, them Dooleys was all sayin' I'd get locked up. I hid out behind our diggings for a week, and then I ran off."

"And you got no kin?"

"No, Pa and me, we was all that was left."

"You can stay with my mother and me until you know what you want to do," Celia told him, her eyes brimming. "We can even give you a job."

"Boy, I'd like that."

"How did your pa die?" Tyler asked.

"He was sick a lot, coughing all the time. And we was never warm enough in that old tent. One mornin' I woke up and he didn't. I buried him in his diggings. There weren't no gold, anyhow."

The boy had tears in his eyes, and looked away.

As evening neared, the storm was even worse, and so Tyler went out, unsaddled the horses, and brought their gear inside. There was no shelter for the animals, and he fretted over it.

They had more of the picnic food for supper, and by then Celia was able to dress in her dry clothes, once more behind Tyler's blanket wall. The boy lay down on his bunk, his dog at his side. Celia put on her gun belt over her skirt and sat down at the table. The boy kept looking at Tyler's vest pocket.

"Do you play that thing, mister?"

After some coaxing, Tyler put the harp between his lips and began to play "Billy Boy," and Celia, feeling warmer and refreshed, began to sing.

The lad smiled and curled up a little more. As she sang, his eyes began to close. She covered the sleeping boy and his dog with a blanket, then sat back down to sing a few more lines as Tyler continued to play. When she was sure the boy was asleep, she stopped singing and Tyler lowered his harmonica.

She gazed sadly from the boy to Tyler, and both were feeling the misery that made the child run away from the mining camp. The storm continued to rage, and Tyler was worried that it might turn to snow.

Celia drew blankets around herself and sat near the hearth, gazing at the flames. Night had fallen and they were all weary.

Neither Tyler nor Celia could forget that unexpected kiss in the rain, but their thoughts were now on Billy. He was all alone, and they would look after him. Tyler suddenly tensed with instinct.

And the door was thrown wide open.

Charging in from the rain was Slap Dooley and a big, bearded man who had to be his brother. The man was as big and ugly as Hop, and both wore slickers. They slammed the door closed and hurried over to the fire. The boy opened his eyes, then turned over and fell asleep again. But the dog was watching.

Celia stood up and backed away to where Tyler was now standing by the table. She moved halfway behind him.

Slap peeled off his slicker and hat and tossed his gear onto the floor. His thin face and evil eyes were set with amusement. "This here's my brother, Jump. Say, did we interrupt somethin'?"

"Hey, it's the kid," Jump said as he spat tobacco juice into the fire. He then pulled off his slicker.

"Leave him alone," Celia said.

Jump's round face was set with a grin, and his dark little eyes narrowed between folds of skin. He touched the scar on his left cheek just above his beard. "Well, he don't count for much, anyhow."

Slap was still amused, and he looked from Celia to Tyler. "How long you two been alone here?"

"We're not alone," Tyler snapped.

"Hey, don't get touchy. Anything to eat here?"

"Fix your own. There's coffee on the hook."

Tyler slowly sat down at the table, and Celia stayed behind him. Jump was looking at them casually, and then he walked over to the shelves, took down a can of beans, and shoved a knife into the lid. He poured them into a pot, spat into the fire again, then knelt to place the pot on the hooks.

Rain was still pounding the roof. The wind was shaking the cabin something fierce, and thunder still rumbled in the night. They seemed isolated from the rest of the world.

While Slap was pouring coffee for them, he continually looked over his shoulder at Tyler and Celia.

"All right," he said, walking to the table with the cups of coffee and sitting opposite Tyler. "We're all gonna be lucky if this cabin doesn't wash right down the hill."

Celia was nervous, and she put her hand on Tyler's shoulder, causing Slap to snicker and grin, while Jump stirred the beans hanging in the hearth.

Then Jump spat again into the fire before he came to sit beside Slap. "What do you think. Slap?"

"I think everything was kind of cozy here."

Tyler stiffened, his left hand turning into a fist on the table, his other hand out of sight. His gaze was intense, his eyes searing. He saw murder in Slap's dark eyes, and he reached up and touched Celia's hand. "Go over to the boy," he murmured.

She walked over to sit with Billy, who still slept.

She stroked the little dog's head, mindful of her gun belt and the Smith & Wesson in her holster.

Jump leaned back in his chair. "Now then, Deputy, it seems you been stickin' your nose in where it ain't wanted."

"That a fact?"

"Mr. Crocker, he allowed as how we oughta tell you to get out of town."

Slap downed his coffee, then let his right hand slip down to his side and out of sight.

Jump put both hands on the table and leaned forward. "So what do you say, Deputy? You gonna make this easy?"

"You mean, if I don't, you'll kill me?"

"Well, now, I figure that's up to you."

"And what about Miss Rollins and the boy? They'd be witnesses."

"Let us worry about that."

At the sound of beans spitting in the pot, Jump got up and walked over to kneel by the hearth, but Tyler kept his eye on Slap, even though he knew Jump was behind him. He prayed Celia could give warning before he was shot in the back. He knew that Slap's right hand was under the table and resting on his holster, the same as Tyler's. Or was Slap's six-gun already drawn and aimed?

Slap's eyes were getting glassy, a sure sign. Suddenly Slap's right shoulder tensed, and Tyler tipped his chair sideways as he drew. He was about to fire when Slap's booming shot cracked past Tyler's thigh and thudded into something solid.

There was a yelp behind Tyler, who spun from his chair and then leaped to his feet, aiming at Slap.

But Slap was rising with shock and agony on his face, his six-gun in his hand, wavering at his side.

All eyes turned to Jump. Slap's bullet had missed Tyler and struck Jump square in the belly. Jump was wild-eyed, heaving and rising with hot pain in his face. He grabbed his belly and staggered backward against the stone hearth, blood running through his fingers.

Tyler stood tense but quiet, his Colt leveled at Slap, who was sliding his weapon into its holster as he staggered toward his dying brother. Slap's face was twisted in horror as he knelt to grab the frantic Jump.

"Jump, I didn't mean it! Jump, I'm sorry!"

Jump jerked and died in his brother's arms, and Slap let the man slide down flat. Face hot with color, half-crazed, Slap stood up and turned slowly, only to stare into Tyler's gun. Tyler strode around the table and spoke gruffly.

"Drop your gun belt with your left hand."

"What for? I missed you, blast it!"

"You're under arrest."

Slap was bleary-eyed. He stared at Tyler's Colt, and he looked over at Celia, who also had her small revolver aimed at him. Billy was sitting on the edge of his bunk and staring.

Slap studied the fury in the deputy's face. Deciding that Tyler would kill him for sure, and still shaken over his brother's death, Slap obeyed, using his unsteady left hand to drop his gun belt.

"Now turn around. Hands behind your back." After holstering his six gun, Tyler took some rawhide strings from Billy, who had jerked them from a hook on the wall. He grabbed Slap's right hand and jerked it down behind him. Then he pulled the left in place and tied his wrists behind his back. Next, Tyler marched him to a bunk at the left wall and shoved him down hard.

"I didn't do nothin' to you," Slap growled.

"You intended to kill me. That's attempted murder of a Federal lawman. Also, you murdered your brother."

"You're loco. No one's goin' to hang a Dooley. Crocker wouldn't stand for it. And everyone else would be too scared. So you may as well let me go."

"We'll see about that when you stand trial."

"What, with Filer? He's just an old justice of the peace. We ain't got no judge, and all they got at the pass is a miner's court, which can't do nothin' here."

"I figure the marshal will know what to do."

"There's my brother there, lyin' in his own blood, and you're blamin' me for it? My gun just went off accidental, that's all."

"Sure, you took it out of the holster for the fun of it."

Slap was exhausted from his anger and frustration. He stretched out on his side, his hands tied behind his back and keeping him mighty uncomfortable.

"Seems to me," Tyler said, "the two of you came up here to kill me and any witnesses. Now that's conspiracy."

"Ain't no such thing, whatever that is. Crocker is my boss, and he won't let me stay locked up."

"That so? Maybe you'll tell me if he paid you to come up here, so I can arrest him."

"I ain't sayin' nothin' against Mr. Crocker. But you got to figure my brother Hop will tear the place apart with his bare hands when he gets back from the mines. And Skip, when he gets back from Denver, he'll shoot you square between the eyes. You might as well face it, you're a dead man."

Tyler knelt to cover Jump's body with two blankets. Then he rose and turned to see Billy back at his bunk and Celia at the fireside. She had rescued the burning beans. Uneasy, she poured herself and Tyler another cup of coffee. As they sat down at the table, they saw that the boy had curled back up with his little dog and was asleep. Soon Slap was snoring.

"Get some sleep," Tyler said to her.

"I can't. You really think they were going to kill all of us? The boy as well?"

"You can bet on it."

Now they heard again the hard rain and wind. Celia sipped her coffee and gazed at Tyler.

"How do you know about the law?"

"My stepfather was a lawyer."

"Was his name Sinclair?"

Tyler nodded and tasted the coffee. It was bitter now, but he drank it just the same. He felt like talking, and she seemed interested.

"Who was your real father?"

"Sinclair was the only father I knew. He let me work in his law office as a clerk from the time I was ten. I learned a lot in four years."

"But you said you ran away. Why?"

Tyler shrugged. "I didn't belong there, that's all. And the war came along. It was a place to go. Lied about my age."

"And your mother?"

"She'd died two years before, when I was twelve."

"How awful for you."

"No worse than your losing your pa and brother."

"Yes, and it's been awful hard on Ma." She looked terribly sad, and then she glanced at the boy. "But I guess it's harder for him."

"Is there another judge besides this Filer?"

"Filer acts as justice of the peace once in a while. There's a real judge in Spanish Bit about thirty miles to the north. But Slap is right. You won't be able to hold him."

"Spanish Bit, huh? Might be worth a visit. But I'd better talk to Ethan."

"What do you think of the marshal?"

"He's all right."

She was thoughtful. "He never takes a drink. Never smokes. He doesn't gamble one bit. He looks at my mother with cow's eyes, but he never goes near her. It's almost as if he's punishing himself."

"For what?"

"I don't know. But you take a good look sometime. It's a wonder he even allows himself any sleep."

"I saw a dime novel about him."

"Really? I'd like to see one. But my father never let us read any of them. He said the devil wrote them." She smiled in memory.

"They do stretch things a mite."

"You know, if you can get the judge to Sweetwater and have a trial, you'd better do it before the Fourth of July. There'd be so many people in town, it would be risky."

"I hear there's a shooting contest. I plan to win that One in a Thousand Winchester."

"I was aimin' for it myself," Celia said.

"I heard you win every year, and maybe you'll win this time.

But how'd you get to be such a good shot?"

"I told you, I was raised in Texas, and I guess it kind of comes natural. Sure makes the fellows mad when I win."

He studied her pride, and he was impressed. "You'd better turn in. I'll keep watch."

"No, I'm wide-awake. You sleep first."

Tyler turned in his chair to look at Slap. "Well, for an hour maybe. But if he stops snoring, you wake me right off."

She nodded, and he stood up slowly, stretching. He lay down on a bunk near the sleeping boy. He drew his six-gun and put it on his belly, keeping it in his right hand. Then he closed his eyes.

Celia waited a few minutes, then went over and put a blanket over Tyler. As she brought it up over his chest, his eyes opened and he looked up at her. She quickly went back to the hearth and put more wood in the fire.

Tyler slept, and Celia paced about. Slap was still snoring. She rested her hand on her revolver where it hung in her holster. She sat down at the table, sipped her coffee, then got up and walked around again.

A few hours before dawn, she was still wide-awake. Tyler was sleeping soundly, but she decided to wake him. She bent over to shake his right shoulder with her left hand, her right hand ready to grip his gun if he was too startled. Her fingers were firm on his shoulder, and his eyes opened. Her flaxen hair was falling about her face, her eyes shining. The firelight made her intensely beautiful.

Tyler raised a hand and slid it behind her back, holding her. They both held their breath as he slowly drew her down. She didn't resist, and her parted lips came an inch from his. He lifted his head and kissed her gently. He felt her shiver under his arm, and he released her.

She drew away from him, her face hot with color, and she stood up, uncertainty still flashing in her eyes. It was then that she saw Billy watching. She went over to him and touched his arm as Tyler got up.

"Go back to sleep, Billy."

The boy closed his eyes, and she moved to where Tyler had been sleeping. She stretched out as he covered her with the blanket. She gazed up at him with a strange look, then closed her eyes.

Tyler realized that it was only a short while to dawn. He helped himself to coffee, and he sat at the table, watching Celia, vowing to stay away from her, yet touched by her beauty and strength.

He thought of Slap and remembered how the man had shoved a gun in his face in the livery. No, Slap wasn't all there, but he was going to hang. Tyler swallowed as he thought of how close they had all come to dying. It pained him that Celia and the boy could have been murdered.

But it wasn't over yet. Listening to the heavy rain, Tyler thought that the beating on the roof was pounding out words, Slap's angry words that kept haunting him: "You may as well face it, Deputy. You're a dead man."

FIVE

*A*FTER a breakfast of beans and thick coffee, Tyler decided to bury Jump then and there. Out in the pouring rain, Tyler and Billy managed a decent burial near the trees, while Celia kept a rifle on the protesting prisoner.

They were soon all mounted, Tyler having added lariats to the saddles in case they had trouble with Slap or the dangerous grade. Water swirled around them, and the wind was tearing at their slickers.

They rode down the steep trail, Tyler in front, followed by the prisoner with his hands tied in front of him and his horse on a long lead to Tyler's. Then came Celia on her mare, and, in the rear, Billy and his dog on the dead man's horse. The heavy rain blinded them off and on, and the horses were often sliding on the wet grass and mud.

To their left, the creek was roaring far below the edge of the cliff-like bank. White foam leaped over rocks, carrying debris and chunks of wood. It sounded like thunder, often so loud that they could hear nothing else.

As they rode huddled in their slickers, Tyler wondered if they were all going to make it back. An hour passed, and there was no way to get away from that terrible drop some ten feet to their left. He wondered how the wagons ever made it.

The rain was heavier and colder, driven by an angry wind. Inches high, water swirled by their horses' hooves.

Slap's evil eyes were narrowed as he hunched down in his slicker, hat pulled down tight, hands gripping the horn. Tyler's horse was suddenly right in front of his mount's nose as they slowed at a bend in the trail.

Slap dug in his heels, and his horse slid into Tyler's, nearly throwing it off the cliff. Tyler's black held its position and spun about, front legs in space as it turned. Slap dug in his heels again, but this time his sorrel tossed its head and backed up crazily.

When the sorrel backed up, it ran into Celia's mare, which slid sideways toward the cliff's edge. She frantically tried to turn it.

"Get off!" Tyler shouted.

The little mare was frightened, and it jumped before Celia could react. Billy urged his sorrel forward, trying to help. Tyler couldn't get around the sneering Slap, and with horror, he saw the mare step into space.

Celia screamed. Her mare was off the cliff, sailing into open air, and they plunged down toward the white water. Celia held on but screamed again.

Tyler grabbed his rope, jumped down, and built a loop. He ran frantically along the cliff's edge, but she was gone from sight.

"Watch Slap!" Tyler shouted to Billy, who pulled a rifle from his saddle scabbard.

Tyler tore off his slicker and leaped right off the cliff into the water with his rope. He sank down into the raging current that swallowed him violently. As he was coming up, a log struck his left shoulder and stunned him for a few moments.

He swam with the current, frantically looking for Celia. His clothes dragged him down. He struck rocks and debris, lost his hat. His boots filled with water and he felt as heavy as stone. He went under several times.

And then he saw her hands, clinging to debris against a rise of rocks, her yellow hair floating as she tried to bring her face up. The strong current kept knocking her under. Her slicker had been torn from her.

Tyler grabbed for her arm. He pulled her up even as he was slammed against the rocks. He turned her about, put her arms about his neck, then put his rope around them both and tied their waists together. They kept going under and swallowing water as he worked, but they would bounce back up as she held again to the debris. Her eyes were wide with fright as she gasped for air.

Tyler looked at the steep banks some thirty feet high on each side with nothing to grab or toss a loop on. The creek was wider here, maybe twenty feet, and over eight feet deep. He knew it would get worse farther on with the deadly rapids.

Now he saw Billy on the cliff's edge. Billy threw a rope again and again until Tyler caught it. Celia was terrified of taking her hand off the debris, but they had to take a chance.

And Billy, his rope around the horn, backed his horse away from the cliff, dragging them through the wild current. They slammed against the rocky wall, and Tyler pulled himself and Celia from the water. She dug her fingers into the wall and clung to the rocks. And soon they were on the cliff's edge, being dragged onto the mud and grass.

There was no sign of Slap or his sorrel.

Billy was on foot now, hurrying to help them to their feet. Celia was shaking from cold, and so weak that she could barely move. She leaned into Tyler's embrace as the rain beat at them.

"Where's Slap?" Tyler asked Billy.

"I had my rifle on 'im, but I couldn't shoot. He took off down the trail. Probably halfway to town by now. I'm real sorry, Tyler."

"It's all right. I'll get him sooner or later."

With his left arm under her knees and his right around her back, Tyler lifted Celia onto his saddle. Then he swung up behind her. She was barely conscious. Billy handed up Tyler's slicker, which he drew about them both.

"Is she gonna die?" Billy asked as he picked up his shivering dog. He put it back on the saddle and mounted.

Tyler didn't answer. Instead, he turned his horse down the trail. Water was pouring over the mud and grass in greater fury than ever. His black had the right experience, but Billy's mount was slipping and nervous.

As they rode down the trail, Tyler could feel Celia going limp in his arms. It was only a few hours to town, but he was worried. She could die before they got there.

When they reached the flats, the bay mare came out of the rushing water like a ghost, eyes wild and nostrils flaring, coughing and snorting for air. It had lost its saddle and bridle, and it stumbled over to fall in behind them.

Billy was amazed. "Tyler, can you believe it?"

"I reckon the Lord wanted that little mare to stick around," Tyler said, equally surprised.

Celia lifted her head with a faint smile.

It was noon when they neared town, and they avoided the flooding from the creek, which was right up to the bridge. They turned and rode into the main street. The rain had turned to sprinkles. The sky was streaked with blue, with the sun shining in spots. A rainbow crossed the foothills toward the pass.

Paxton came out of the jail and paused, startled.

"Where's the doc?" Tyler asked.

"Last white house on your right."

"Where's Ethan?"

"North side."

Tyler rode on to the doctor, and he sent Billy to get Maggie. The wiry doctor made room on a bed in his office and Celia was stretched out as Tyler pulled off her slicker. She was unconscious.

"You didn't get here any too soon," the doctor said.

Tyler stood a moment, heart pounding, but he turned just as Maggie and Billy rushed inside. Maggie was frantic. She hugged Celia and felt her burning face.

"You were both foolish to go up there with a storm coming," Maggie said.

Tyler felt guilty as he carried Celia into a back room where Maggie could help the doctor get rid of her wet clothes. Then the doctor chased him and Billy out of the office. "Come back tomorrow," he ordered.

Uneasy, Tyler left, and found the horses being cared for at the livery. Paxton greeted him, and said, "From what that boy tells me, you saved her life."

"Her mother was right. Never should have gone up there."

"You couldn't know the storm would come this way."

But Tyler felt plenty guilty. And he felt bad about losing a prisoner. It would be hard to explain to Ethan. As he entered the jailhouse, he saw Billy and his dog sound asleep on his bunk.

Ethan was sitting at his desk, and he looked up. "You'd better get out of them wet clothes."

Tyler sat down near the stove, so weary that he felt his body would crack apart. In silence, he changed to dry clothes, but he remained cold. He poured himself some coffee and sat down near the desk, feeling awkward.

"Reckon I lost my prisoner."

"Billy told me what happened. You all could have been killed. But it seems you saved that girl's life."

"We should have stayed in the cabin."

"More of Crocker's men might have come. And with that flooding, no tellin' if the cabin's even there now. You made the right decision."

Tyler was grateful for Ethan's words, and he sipped his coffee. "Once I get some sleep, I'll go after Slap."

"I'll go with you, but right now, take my bunk."

"We got to protect Celia and the boy."

Ethan nodded. "No tellin' what the Dooleys will do. Slap's got two brothers left. They all have Crocker behind 'em."

"I don't care who's out there. Slap Dooley's going to be locked up."

Ethan frowned, leaned back, and put his feet on his desk. "There's the judge over in Spanish Bit, and we could try to get Slap over there. But once we're out in the open, we're dead. That's assuming we even find Slap."

"So we got to do something different."

74

"I figure we'll send for the judge right now while Slap is figurin' he won't get caught."

"You think Slap is halfway out of the country?"

"No. They're too arrogant. He'll be around somewhere."

Suddenly, the door burst open and Crocker was standing there, his face pink and his big jaw jutting outward. He stormed inside, slammed the door behind him, and glared at Tyler.

"I heard you killed Jump Dooley. What for?" Ethan put his feet down and turned. "You got it backward, Crocker. Slap killed his own brother."

"What?"

"He tried to kill my deputy, but he missed and got Jump."

Crocker digested it all for a while, and then he seemed to take hold of himself. "Well, where's Slap?"

"If you ain't seen him," Tyler said, "how'd you know Jump was dead?"

"I got my ways of knowin' things!"

"Seems like Slap's been telling you a pack of lies," Tyler said. "You go tell him I'll be over when I'm good and ready."

Crocker moistened his lips. "I don't know where Slap is, but Hop should be back from the mines by tonight. And Skip, any day now, will be back from

Denver. Now you can tell any story you want, but the Dooleys are going to blow your head off, Deputy."

"Since they work for you," Ethan said, "I reckon you'll have to make sure they don't get in our way. In fact, I'm holdin' you responsible."

"Oh, no, you don't. I can't do nothin' about it."

"We get any trouble from your men, I'm coming after you, Crocker."

75

Enraged, Crocker strode from the room and slammed the door behind him. Ethan shook his head and got up to get some coffee off the stove. He poured Tyler a cup too, then returned to his desk.

Abruptly, the door opened again and Maggie entered. She wore a small hat and a long coat over her green outfit. Her eyes were red from crying, and she was badly shaken.

"I was waitin' for that awful man to leave," she said. "Now then, Tyler Sinclair, I want to talk to you." Both men got to their feet. As she walked right up to Tyler and gazed at him strangely, he knew that she was blaming him for Celia's terrible experience.

But she extended her arms and hugged him. Tyler was so startled that he could only stare down at her.

Then she backed away and said, "I just wanted to thank you. My daughter's going to be all right. And she tells me you saved her life."

Tyler was embarrassed. "Any man would have done the same."

"No," she argued. "Except for Ethan, I don't know any other man that foolish."

She gave him a lovely smile that Tyler would never forget. Then she was gone as abruptly as she had come, leaving a silence that hung over the two men for a long while. Finally, Ethan grinned.

"Well, son, you're now a hero."

Tyler shrugged. "Maybe you ought to call me Tyler."

"Bothers you, does it? I reckon callin' you 'son' comes natural, because you're young enough to be my son. And if I had one, I figure I'd want him to be just like you."

Tyler couldn't answer. He had mixed emotions—joy at the compliment and agony at wondering if he should be hating Ethan. He had known him only a matter of days, and already he wanted Ethan for a friend.

But Tyler's curiosity was painful, and he heard himself ask the question, "You ever been to Kentucky?"

"Nope," Ethan said, turning away.

The answer stunned Tyler. He was both sorry and glad. So this man could not be his father if he were being truthful. Still shaken, Tyler was almost sorry he had asked the question.

Weary and aching, he went to Ethan's bunk and stretched out. With eyes closed, he mouthed a silent prayer of thanks that Celia would live. He fell asleep, but a few minutes later, he was awake enough to realize that Ethan was covering him with a blanket.

* * *

While Tyler was sleeping, his friend Shorty from the Hawkens spread was down on the flats, heading north. In his vest pocket was a letter for Tyler. It was from Kentucky.

SIX

AFTER Tyler had some sleep and two men were dispatched to Spanish Bit, he and Ethan and Billy went to the hotel for supper. On the way back, they stopped at the Rollins freight office. Maggie was inside at her desk, wearing a blue dress with lace at the collar. There was no sign of Celia.

Seated in front of her desk was a heavy man in a black coat and little string tie. His lean face was smooth, and he had a skinny nose and gray eyes that were nearly white. His teeth kept flashing in a politician's smile. It was obvious that he had come to call on Maggie.

Standing near the man was a younger edition, with the same face and clothes but also with a fancy gold watch and chain and a great deal of arrogance.

"Mr. Percy Filer," Maggie said. "You know the marshal. This is his deputy, Tyler Sinclair, and our friend Billy. Mr. Filer owns the bank and the livery, and some of the stores, and the hotel. This here's his son, Peter."

Percy Filer stood up and shook their hands. But his son

merely snickered and said, "Well, Tyler, I hear you're quite a hero. Seems to me you were just plain lucky."

"Luck it was," Tyler admitted.

"Nonsense," Maggie said. "He risked his life to save Celia. And Billy helped too. He pulled them out of the creek."

"Some storm," Percy said. "We nearly lost the bridge again."

"How's Celia?" Tyler asked.

Immediately, Peter came forward. "She's sleeping. Had to break our supper date, thanks to you."

Tyler met the man's glare with a tough look. So this dandy saw him as competition. Peter didn't know how scared Tyler was of women.

"Billy needs a place to stay," Ethan told Maggie.

Maggie smiled. "He's welcome here. And so's the puppy."

"But you got to know," the lawman added. "Him and Celia are witnesses, and it may not be safe for 'em."

"Don't you worry," she said. "Anyone comes around, I'll blow their brains out."

Ethan had to grin. "Now, that's no way for a lady to talk."

Maggie and Ethan gazed at each other for a while. Percy Filer looked back and forth between them, his eyes growing wider. Then Ethan suggested to her, "Maybe Mr. Filer could put you up at his house."

"I've offered," Percy said.

She shook her head. "No, Ethan. We got men workin' for us. When they get back from the mines, we'll keep a few around."

"And I can shoot," Billy said. Then he flushed and hugged his pup as he remembered he'd been unable to stop Slap.

"Don't you worry," Tyler assured the boy. "When it's necessary to save a life, you'll pull the trigger."

Billy looked relieved. Tyler glanced at the back room door, wishing he could see Celia for himself. And the door suddenly opened.

Celia came out in a dressing gown with a blanket wrapped around her. Her hair was spun gold in the lamplight, and it spilled down her shoulders and around her throat. She looked so pretty that Tyler had to swallow, and she was looking only at him.

"Tyler Sinclair, don't you dare leave without seeing me."

"Uh, I'm glad you're all right."

She crossed the room, unmindful of everyone else, and stood on her tiptoes, her hand sliding up his chest to his neck. She pulled his head down so she could kiss his weathered cheek. Then she drew back with a smile, her eyes glistening.

"Thank you, Tyler. You saved my life."

He was mighty uncomfortable. "You and Billy have got to stay inside. You're witnesses, and they'd just as soon you were dead."

She wasn't worried. "We're all good shots in here." Peter went over to her and took her hand. "Celia, I was so worried about you. Now, you rest up. Tomorrow night we'll have that supper date."

Color danced on her face. "Of course, Peter." Percy Filer cleared his throat. "Well, Maggie, at least three of us can go on to supper, and we're late. The chef is preparing a special meal for us."

Maggie glanced at Ethan. "I'm not very hungry, Percy."

But Percy insisted and escorted her outside. Peter hesitated, looking back and forth between Celia and Tyler. He was obviously worried, but he followed his father and Maggie out into the night.

Billy watched the door close behind them and frowned. Celia sat on the edge of the desk, keeping her blanket close around her as she smiled at the boy. "I'm glad you're here, Billy."

Billy walked over and touched her arm. "Me too." Ethan and Tyler said good-bye and went out into the darkness. Pausing on the boardwalk, Ethan watched Maggie and the Filers heading toward the hotel. Then

Ethan's chest tightened when Percy Filer picked her up and carried her across the muddy street.

"Looks bad," Tyler said. "You'd better be saying your piece."

Ethan grunted. "What about you? That's a mighty pretty girl in there. Pete Filer and half the town's been courting her."

"She's pretty, all right, but she thinks I killed her brother. Besides, I learned a long time ago that women just can't be trusted. They don't know how to be faithful."

"That's a strong statement for a young man."

"I ain't so young."

They headed north, both silent as they thought of the danger they were facing. Ambush would be easy on the other side. False fronts, alleys, so many merchants owing too much to Crocker. There were no friends over there.

"First place we'll look," Ethan said, "is the Wild Card Saloon, which belongs to Crocker. The Dooleys bunk in the sheds behind the freight office. That's the next place."

"When we hit the saloon, someone will warn 'em."

"They know we're comin'. Besides, ain't likely they'd bunk down this early. The Dooleys like whiskey and cards. But I don't figure Hop is back. It's gonna be Slap by hisself."

"You don't think he'll be hiding?"

"He's too arrogant."

As they neared the livery, Paxton came out with a rifle and said, "I'm comin' along."

Ethan shook his head. "It ain't necessary."

"Marshal, there's a rifle behind every door over there."

"If something happens to us, someone's got to take over here. I gave you that part-time job as a deputy for that very reason. But I'd be mighty appreciative if you'd watch the bridge. We may need cover gettin' back."

Paxton nodded, but was disappointed.

Tyler and Ethan continued to the office, where they picked up shotguns and handcuffs. Then they headed toward the bridge. It was cold and damp, and the muddy road still ran with water. There were some clouds in the night sky. A half-moon was rising and stars were beginning to twinkle. Ahead was a deadly town, silent and waiting.

They crossed the bridge, boots clunking on wood. The creek here was wide and shallow normally, but the water was high to the boards and white with foam, gleaming in the pale light.

There were some horses at the railings, but no people were in sight. The dance halls were dark, but the saloons had lamps burning inside and soft light reached out. There was no music. They heard no laughter as they moved up the muddy street. It was as if everything was muffled.

The pale moonlight cast their shadows before them as they moved onto the boardwalk. Now their boots could be heard as they neared the first saloon.

But they passed it and the dark dance hall, moving on to the Wild Card Saloon, two buildings before the freight office.

The lawmen could hear their hearts pounding. Their boots clunked on the wood as they neared the Wild Card.

It was as if the streets had been cleared, just waiting to swallow them up. They knew that at any minute, a bullet could hit them square between the eyes, or in the back.

Tyler went in through the swinging doors of the Wild Card, while Ethan went through the alley and around to the back.

Tyler held the shotgun waist high and level as he entered. Five men were playing cards at a table by the right wall. The wiry bartender was serving three men at the bar. There was no one else in sight.

Tyler moved to the left, keeping his back to the wall as he came slowly forward. The men at the bar darted aside and over toward the cardplayers. Leaning on the bar, Tyler looked grimly at the barkeep and asked, "You seen Slap Dooley around here?"

"Nope."

Tyler aimed the shotgun at him, and the man started sweating. "You sure?"

"Look, mister, I got nothin' to say."

Suddenly, shots rang out in the back, one the blast of a shotgun. Tyler charged around the bar and to the back door. He kicked it open and ran out into the night. He heard more shots as he ran toward the corrals behind the freight office. Suddenly he stumbled over the bodies of two mean-looking fellows, one hit with a shotgun that had torn his chest open.

Then Tyler saw a figure jump the corral fence, and Ethan was stumbling along in the mud, heading after him with the shotgun in his left hand and his six-gun in his right. Tyler caught up with him and whispered: "Ethan, you been hit?"

"Twice, but we got 'im on the run. You go to the left."

"Is he alone?"

"He is now. It was a trap."

Tyler hurried to the left, where the horses were being bunched up at one end. He knelt by the fence and looked through the shadowed, moving legs of the animals. He saw a gleam of steel, and he set down his shotgun and drew his six-gun.

As Tyler leaped the fence, a bullet whistled by his ear. He landed in the middle of the nervous horses and dropped to one knee. Then he crawled through the horses, their hooves flying near his head.

He saw a man throwing a saddle on a horse, and it sure looked like Slap. Tyler got to his feet and went running through the horses. Slap spun around and fired. The bullet grazed the side of Tyler's head, stunning him.

Still, Tyler didn't want to kill Slap. He wanted him alive. When he saw the man in the saddle, he charged forward, right into another bullet that cut through his left arm.

Slap reined the horse about, trying to run over Tyler. Tyler leaped aside and, grabbing Slap by the right arm, jerked him high and clear of the saddle. Slap fell down into the mud as his horse jumped away.

Crazed, Slap rose to one knee and fired at Tyler. But he missed. Tyler sprang forward and slammed his fist in the man's face. Slap went over backward, firing on an empty shell. Tyler jerked the gun from his hand, grabbed him by the bandanna, and hauled him to his feet.

"You're under arrest!" he roared.

Slap cursed and kicked as Tyler spun him around and cuffed his hands behind his back. Tyler slammed him against the fence, then took up the reins of the saddled horse. He shoved Slap through the corral gate, led the horse out, and closed the gate behind them. Then he marched Slap toward where Ethan might be.

He stumbled on Ethan in the dark, lying on his back, bleeding from his chest and side. Tyler helped him sit up and rise to his feet.

"Come on, Ethan, you got to get on the horse."

"I'll try."

Tyler almost had to lift the lawman into the saddle. Then he took the lariat from the saddle and put the noose around Slap's neck while Slap continued to curse him.

Tyler gave the reins to Ethan, but he held on to the bridle strap and started the horse moving around the corrals. The sheds and bunkhouse were silent and dark. There was no sign of anyone.

Slap was still crazed. "You just wait. That tin star's gonna be shoved down your throat. And I'm gonna do it myself."

Tyler shoved him on ahead, the noose scratching Slap's skinny neck. There was no easy way to avoid the street and still get to the bridge. He prayed that Slap had only two friends, both dead.

Ethan was bent over the pommel, barely able to keep astride. The moon seemed even brighter.

Tyler kept shoving Slap on ahead, the noose slowly tightening. They were fifty feet from the bridge now, and there was no sign of Paxton.

Breath tight in his lungs, Tyler moved faster, and he kept glancing at Ethan, who was sure to fall out of the saddle before long.

Suddenly, shots rang out, one cutting through Tyler's hat, another hitting Ethan in the saddle. Tyler spun and could see the flash of lights in the alley. He fired, then ran behind the horse and slammed his fist on its rump.

The horse broke into a lope, springing for the bridge as Ethan fought to stay astride. It darted across, bullets sailing past the lawman as he swayed in the saddle.

Tyler grabbed Slap and pulled him up against his side, marching him close and fast. Maybe they wouldn't take a chance on hitting Slap. And Tyler was right. He made it to the bridge, but Slap suddenly shoved him away with his shoulder.

Bullets rang out from the side of the last saloon near the bridge, but Paxton's rifle barked twice. Tyler looked back to see two men staggering to their knees and rolling over in the mud.

Paxton came running past Tyler and his prisoner, and he went over the bridge and looked at the dead briefly. Then he came back and caught up with Tyler. They were followed by silence from the north side.

"Don't know them," Paxton muttered, "but Crocker gets a lot of new faces. I think he's runnin' a hideout over there."

At the jail, Ethan had managed to haul the horse to a stop, and he had fallen off and into the mud, bleeding from three bullet wounds. While Paxton took charge of the prisoner, Tyler ran over to the lawman.

"Ethan, can you hear me?"

"Just get me inside, son."

Tyler hauled him to his knees and pulled him onto the boardwalk and into the office. He turned up the wall lamps and then carried Ethan to his bunk.

Paxton locked up the prisoner and then ran for the doctor. Tyler knelt by Ethan and tried to pull open his shirt. Blood was flowing through Tyler's fingers. He was terrified that Ethan was going to die, and he forgot his own wounds.

Ethan's face was void of color. He looked like he was going fast. Tyler shook him.

"You can't die on me," he said. "I got to know."

Ethan was gazing at him with a blank expression.

Tyler had tears in his eyes. "I got to know, Ethan. Are you my pa?"

Ethan just gazed at him with an odd, faded expression. Tyler was frantic. He pressed his bandanna on one of the wounds and Ethan's on another. Still the blood flowed. Tyler's left arm was caked with his own blood, but he felt no pain.

"Ethan, you can't die on me. I got to know."

Ethan's eyes closed, and Tyler shook him again. Tears trickled down Tyler's hardened face. His eyes were burning, and he slowly relaxed his hands, finding his fingers numb.

"Blast it, Ethan!" he muttered, sitting back, choking on his tears. "I was born to Angela Mandell back in Kentucky. My father left a month after the wedding and never came back. His name was Ethan Mandell, and I ain't never found that name on anyone until now."

The words hung in the silence, but the lawman just lay there bleeding, eyes closed. Tyler knelt beside him. Then he swallowed hard, his voice wavering. "Ethan," he said gently, "they said my father was bad and run off. I got to know if it was you, and if it *was*, why you left her and me. I know that her brother was killed, but why run away if it was a fair fight? Why didn't you write?"

Ethan didn't move. He was barely alive. Tyler wiped his tears from his face and kept mumbling his words.

"I hated my father, and if it's you, Ethan, I got to know. She had him declared dead, and she married Sinclair when I was seven. She didn't care about me one bit. No one did. Ethan, if you're my pa, I got to know if you knew about me and if you cared."

Ethan wasn't moving. Tyler's words echoed in his own ears, and he bent his head and whispered a silent prayer. His heart was sick, his stomach churning. He had felt abandoned from birth by both of his parents. Now he was a grown man and crying like a child.

"She didn't care about my father at all. As far back as I can remember, she had men all around her, and she was always flirting and lying to them. I still remember that nice big fellow sitting on the porch, crying like a baby because she had teased him on and then turned him down. I ain't never trusted a woman since." He wiped at his tears, but Ethan appeared lifeless, and Tyler's words kept spilling from his quivering lips.

"The whole time, she hated my father. And both her family and Sinclair's were always saying how I had bad blood. I was always fighting with the other boys. And when I beat three of them up pretty bad, that's when I ran away. I ain't never been back."

He sat on his heels, unable to stop crying. He feared Ethan would die before he ever learned the truth. But he had to take hold of himself before Paxton returned with the doctor. Maybe some coffee would help.

Tyler was about to rise when he saw a tear trickling down Ethan's cheek. The lawman's lips moved, but no sound came. Tyler leaned close.

"Ethan, are you my father?"

Slowly, Ethan's heavy lids moved, and the wet gray-blue eyes were fixed on Tyler. More tears trickled down the lawman's face. He tried to talk, and finally his words came, hoarse and barely audible:

"I didn't know about you."

"You're my pa? You were in Kentucky?"

Ethan nodded. His eyes closed again. "Couldn't go back."

"But you said you'd never been to Kentucky."

"Didn't want anyone to know."

Tyler swallowed hard, choking on his tears. A crazy grin came to his face, and he gripped the lawman by both arms, desperate to hug him.

"You *are* my father!"

Both men were weeping freely, and Tyler put his face on the man's chest, in his blood, and then he felt the lawman go limp. Tyler straightened, frantic. "Blast you, Ethan! You'd better not die on me!" He shook the man, but Ethan was unconscious. Tyler turned as the door opened and the doctor came running inside, followed by Paxton and Maggie. She was still in her fancy dress, and Percy Filer came along behind them. The banker looked annoyed at the whole thing.

Tyler stood up, wiped away his tears and the blood, and turned toward the stove. As the doctor worked on Ethan, Tyler built up the fire, trying to keep busy. All these years he had hated a ghost, but he knew now that he could never hate this man.

He turned and looked at the odd expression on Paxton's face, at the tearful Maggie wringing her hands, at the angry Percy, who stayed by the door. Sitting down, Tyler watched the doctor try to stop the bleeding. It seemed hours before the doctor turned and stood up, his clothes covered with blood. Then he and Maggie came over to the stove to warm their hands.

"Well, Doc?" Tyler asked, frantic.

"He's lost too much blood. He won't last till morning."

Tyler went limp in his chair. "Can't you do anything?"

"I stopped the bleeding, but he's hurt bad. Still got one bullet in him, but no use trying to get it out now."

"What can I do for him?"

"Keep him warm. And say a prayer for him."

"With Slap Dooley in a cell back there, it's dangerous," Maggie said. "We got to get the marshal to where he'll be safe."

The doctor shook his head. "Ethan hasn't a chance, and moving him would make that for sure. Let him die in peace."

The doctor patched Tyler's arm where the bullet had gone clean through, and cleaned off his head where it had been creased. Then the doctor marched Maggie to the door, where Percy Filer put on his best smile and escorted her outside. Tyler just sat staring at the dying man.

"Listen," Paxton said. "I don't know exactly what's going on, but you got to know we're in trouble now. Just you and me holdin' Slap back there. The judge will be another day gettin' here. This town is loaded with dynamite. And all of Crocker's men are just on the other side of that bridge."

Tyler wiped his eyes. "Crocker?"

"He keeps his men because he stands by 'em, so he's got to get Slap out. And he wants the whole town back. He was runnin' it afore Rollins and the others started buildin' up on the south side. Crocker's got a lot of shady fellows over there, and he'll have plenty of help."

"So what's next?"

"You get some sleep. I'll wake you about two."

"We may not be gettin' out of here alive—is that it?"

Paxton shrugged. "Well, we'll give it a try. Meanwhile, Ethan has plenty of grub, coffee, and water in here. And plenty of ammunition. So we ain't goin' nowhere."

Tyler gathered one of his blankets and walked over to Ethan. He spread it on the floor and lay down next to his father's bunk. At long last he slept, but fitfully.

When Paxton awakened Tyler at two in the morning, Ethan was as white as snow and barely breathing. Tyler had a cup of coffee, then sat near his father, arms folded. Paxton went to sleep on Tyler's bunk and was soon snoring softly.

Tyler scrunched up, legs Indian fashion, and he pulled his blanket around him. Hours passed. Just before dawn, he gazed at his father again, and then bowed his head.

"Lord," he said softly, "I ain't never asked You for anything, You know that. All them times with cannons blowing my friends out of the grass and blood all over me. And back in the stampede in Texas when I was run over. I figured You had better things to worry about. But I'm begging You now, Lord. Please let him live."

His voice sounded strange in the silence of the jailhouse. He couldn't cry anymore, but he was sure hurting.

A minute later, as Tyler got up to go for more coffee, a hand came to rest on his shoulder. It startled him so much that he nearly cried out. He turned. It was Ethan's hand, and he was gazing at him. Finally he whispered:

"I'm glad you're my son. I'm right proud."

Tyler swallowed. "Doggone it, you can't die on me."

"I'm workin' on it."

"You hurting bad?"

"Like sin. Pain feels like a knife."

"Then you're gonna live."

"Maybe so."

Awakened by the voices, Paxton rose on his elbow. And then he grinned and said, "You all right, Ethan?"

"I ain't sure. Where's Slap?"

"He's in the cell out back, madder'n a wet hornet." Ethan tried to rise, but Tyler pushed him back, saying, "Listen, Pa, you—"

For a moment, Tyler's words were as stunning to him as they were to Paxton. Ethan managed a weak grin. Then Tyler grinned back.

"Let me sleep," Ethan said.

"Not a chance. I'm gonna pour coffee into you."

"Your coffee burns my gut."

"Good."

Tyler got up and went for the coffee while Paxton rushed off for the doctor.

Tyler turned his father on his side to sip the coffee. "Ethan, I'm glad you're my father. I hated a ghost for so long, but I know now I was wrong. Ma's family said a lot of bad things about you, and like a fool, I believed it all."

Ethan tasted the coffee, then let his head roll back. "Son, they weren't that far off. I was a wild one. I fell for your ma all right, but once we was hitched, everything went wrong. They tried to change me. Wanted to run my life, make me into a gentleman, make me perfect. I didn't feel like a man anymore. I got back at 'em by gambling and drinking."

"And her brother?"

"He was rotten clean through, but he had the family name, you know, and they were society. He was always cheating at cards, and one day I caught him red-handed. He drew and I shot him. That's all. There were witnesses. But he was your ma's favorite. She hated me for it and ran me off with some ugly words. There was no going back after that."

Tyler swallowed hard. "So you didn't know she was pregnant."

"No, son, I swear. We'd only been married a few weeks. You got to figure she didn't know it herself."

"If they didn't like you none, how come you got to marry her in the first place?"

Ethan grinned in pain. "Listen here, son, I was a mighty handsome fellow."

"Pa, maybe you'd better stop talking."

"I got to, son. I may not make it."

Tyler was frantic and helped him sip more coffee. Ethan gazed up at Tyler. "I'm right sorry I never knew you afore. All those years wasted."

"I'll be twenty-nine on the Fourth."

Ethan shook his head slowly. "Glory be. You got to tell me everything, Tyler. All you done all your life."

"First off, you don't have to feel bad about leaving Ma. As far back as I can remember, men were calling on her. She was always laughing and having a good time. She'd promise her love to one, then turn her back and say the same thing to another. And each time you'd swear it was the truth. But she waited until she got Sinclair, because he had the most money."

"I don't remember him."

"He came along later. Got to be the family lawyer. About a year ago I wrote a letter to tell him where I was. Don't know what got into me. I guess I was lonesome for family. But I don't care if I never hear from him, now that I found you."

"We're gonna be together from now on, son. But right now, blast, I hurt."

Tyler gripped his arm. "You're gonna be fine. I seen how you was looking at Maggie. Ma died of a fever when I was twelve. You've been a free man for seventeen years."

"I wish I'd known."

Tyler told how the other youths in the family taunted him, how no one wanted him around, including his mother. He related how he worked in the law office for Sinclair, but ran off after he beat up three of his cousins when they came at him. He told of the war and of how he had learned to ride and rope and herd cattle in Texas.

"But I never could get close to a woman," Tyler went on. "I was always afraid they'd be like Ma. When I got to Texas, I got real friendly with one girl down in Austin, and she was talking like we were going to get hitched. But when I saw her flirting with other men behind my back, I just saddled up and rode away."

"All women ain't the same, son."

And Ethan told him bits and pieces about his roaming, his Army days fighting Apaches, and how he became a lawman. But he had never felt he was a free man, and so he stayed away from women.

Tyler retrieved the dime novel and showed it to him. Ethan had to grin while groaning in pain at the same time.

"So he really wrote it, huh? I met that fellow down in Tombstone. By golly, the picture even looks a little like me."

"When you're up to it, I'll read it to you. Made you out to be quite a hero."

Ethan looked up with a tear in his eye. "You want to know about heroes? My son took on Hop Dooley, knowin' he could be killed, just because of an insult to his father."

Tyler was tickled. "Well, I guess I was being a bit of a hothead."

"Made me proud, and I didn't even know who you were."

There was a pounding at the door and Tyler removed the bar, admitting Paxton, the doctor, and Maggie. Paxton was carrying a sack of grub, and Maggie had a kettle of soup that she handed to Tyler. Then she pushed in front of the doctor, knelt by Ethan, and placed her cool hand on his brow.

"Ethan Mandell, you're such a bother."

Ethan opened his eyes and gazed at her fondly. "Maybe you ought to do something about it." He lifted a weak hand, reaching to enclose her slim fingers. "I need you."

She was startled. "Ethan?"

"I'm a free man, Maggie. I just found it out." Maggie was bright with understanding as she smiled. Love was written all over her face. She squeezed Ethan's hand. There were tears in her eyes.

The doctor pushed her aside. "Won't do you no good, Ethan, if you die on us. Now lie still."

Maggie staggered to her feet, tears trickling down her face. She looked at Tyler, who took her arm and led her over to the stove. He showed her the dime novel.

"Oh, Tyler," she whispered, "I love that man."

"He's my pa, Maggie."

"What?"

She stared up at him, then hugged him. The doctor rose to his feet and said, "I gave him something for the pain."

Maggie stormed over to him. "Now, you listen to me, Doc. He'd better live or you're not gettin' any more home-cooked meals at my house."

The doctor made a face. "I didn't think he'd last the night, but he's a tough one."

Then she half knelt by Ethan's bunk, drew up his mustache, and kissed him square on the lips. He gazed at her with adoration. Smiling, she rose and looked with embarrassment at the others. After dressing Tyler's arm, the doctor marched her toward the door as he spoke:

"If he gets a fever, you call me. And if he improves, maybe I can take that bullet out by tonight. Come along, Maggie."

"I'm staying."

"Please go with the doctor," Tyler said. "And keep Billy and your daughter locked up. No telling when trouble will explode."

He walked her and the doctor to the door, but she hesitated just outside and turned to gaze at Tyler. "Take care of him, please."

Tyler nodded. He barred the door and turned, seeing a silly smile on Ethan's face. Tyler slid the dime novel back in his war bag, then knelt at Ethan's side. "Maggie is a woman in a million," Tyler said.

Ethan nodded. "I got a lot of love for her. But I can see I got to trim back this mustache."

Tyler pulled a chair over and sat next to him. Paxton brought Ethan the hot soup, then lay down on Tyler's bunk.

"Listen, son," Ethan began, and then nearly choked on the soup as he smiled. "Sounds good, doesn't it?"

"So you never suspected who I was."

"No. I was sure I knew you from somewhere, though. Maybe

I was seein' myself. But I just shut my mind to it. I certainly liked you right off."

"Where do we go from here?"

"I got me a son, and I give thanks for that. Maybe when this is all over, we'll find us a new life. I've been wearing a badge and pushing my luck too long."

"What about Maggie?"

"I'd like her to come along, if she'll have me."

"Whatever we do, I'd like it mighty fine."

Ethan touched his hand. "Now I want to sleep awhile. But you play your mouth harp, will you?"

"Listen, Pa, we got to get you out of here before they come after Slap. Hop could be back anytime."

"I ain't goin' nowhere."

"If you stay here, you'll just get hurt."

They heard Paxton chuckle, and they grinned at each other. Ethan couldn't get hurt much worse than he was already, so Tyler just gave up and Ethan closed his eyes.

Later, Paxton went out and made excursions up and down the street. But there was no sign of trouble, although the north side was surprisingly silent. That night, the doctor came to take out the bullet.

While Ethan was being treated, Hop Dooley was riding into the corrals on the north side of town. The two wagons loaded with shipments from the mine were ahead of him and the three other exhausted men.

"I thought we'd never get back from there," one man said. "In fact, I figured by now we'd be drowned in that blasted creek."

Hop grunted. "We made it. And I sure need somethin' to eat. But I'd better go see Crocker first."

In Crocker's office, Hop pushed his hat back from his dirty face. He was sweaty and tired, and his big belly poked out of his shirt between the buttons. Crocker was sitting behind his huge desk, his fancy carved pipe in his mouth, and his hand smoothing his blond hair.

"We got two wagons of ore out there, Mr. Crocker. Got to get 'em to the smelter at Spanish Bit. But with you plannin' to build a smelter north of town, our trips will sure be a lot shorter, eh?"

Crocker nodded and tapped his pipe. But he didn't answer.

Hop became annoyed. "I figured you'd be pleased, what with us beatin' Rollins. Them women can't do much with your big loads."

"I am pleased. And I'll be payin' Filer back sooner than expected."

"Pretty soon it'll be the Fourth. I think I'll spend the next couple of days practicin'. I sure aim to win that rifle. If Skip ain't back by then, I'll get it sure." Crocker spoke abruptly. "Jump is dead."

"What?"

"Your brother is dead."

Hop was on the edge of his chair. "How?"

"I paid him and Slap to ride up to the relay cabin and get rid of Tyler Sinclair. Slap tried to gun 'im, but he missed and got Jump instead. Celia Rollins and a boy saw it happen."

Hop wiped his brow. "Where's Slap?"

"In jail. They ought to have the judge here by tomorrow sometime."

"Poor old Jump. But I don't want Slap in that jail. And I don't want him seein' no judge."

Crocker leaned back, puffing on his pipe. "So what do you plan to do?"

"I'm gettin' him out, and you're gonna help me."

"I have some boys lined up. What you got to do is get rid of both them tin badges while you're at it. Then maybe we can get our town back."

"And the witnesses?"

Crocker smiled. "Kill 'em."

SEVEN

At the Rollins stage office late that night, Maggie was pacing back and forth. "I wish that doctor would have let me go to the jail with him," she said.

Celia was sitting on the edge of the desk, and Billy was behind the desk, in Maggie's chair. The little pup was playing with Celia's boot and trying to bite it.

"Now, Mama," Celia said, "you know they ordered us to stay in the office here. I just wish some of the boys would get back."

"There's gonna be a big fight," Billy said.

Maggie frowned. "I sure hope not. But when all is said and done, and all the wash hung out, maybe we'll find out who killed Pa and Jody."

Billy stood up. "I'll help."

"And why aren't you in bed asleep?" Maggie asked him.

"Aw, Maggie, I ain't sleepy."

There was a pounding on the back door, at the end of the hallway that led to the tack room and the corrals.

"Must be the boys," Maggie said. "They sure are late."

Celia nodded. "I'll go."

"Make sure they rub down them mules. They weren't too careful last time. We can't afford any lame stock. And you tell Jed to bring the boys around in the morning for their pay."

Celia nodded and went down the long hallway to the back door. She drew a heavy shawl about her shoulders as she opened it and entered the room full of harnesses and saddles. She turned up the hanging lamps. The pounding continued at the outside door, and a man's muffled voice called out:

"It's Jed. Open up."

"I didn't hear no wagons," Billy said to Maggie, and he reached for a rifle that rested against the wall.

But Celia was already removing the bar from the outside door, and she swung it open. Lantern light framed her in the doorway as she peered out, seeing no one.

Billy came running down the hallway with the rifle. But it was too late. A big hand had closed on Celia's arm, another over her mouth, muffling her scream as she was jerked into the night. The door slammed shut behind her.

Celia was lifted like a child. The big fat hand hurt her mouth, and she squealed and fought as Hop Dooley carried her in his arms through the corrals at a run.

Billy jerked the door open and yelled, "Hey, Celia! Where are you?"

But he saw only darkness. He ran out into the corral and looked around frantically. He knew that a terrible thing had happened.

Maggie came running outside, a six-gun in her hand. "What is it? What's wrong? Where is everybody?"

"It weren't Jed, Maggie. Someone got Celia."

Maggie gasped. "Oh, no! We've got to get the marshal!"

"He's bad hurt. It's Tyler we need."

"Don't you see, Billy? They want to trade Celia for Slap, and the marshal got no right to do that."

They stood in the cold night, deep in mud, helpless and frightened. Then Billy ran to the fence and climbed over.

"I'll get Tyler."

"No, Billy, you're a witness. It's not safe."

But Billy was already over the second fence and running up the street. When he reached the jailhouse, he gasped for air as he pounded on the door. Tyler let him inside.

Billy staggered over to a chair and sat down. Finally catching his breath, he spoke in a frenzy:

"They got Miss Celia. Maggie says it's 'cause they want to trade her for Slap."

Tyler was badly shaken, and he sat down at the desk, his stomach churning. Celia a prisoner, a witness they wanted dead, being offered as a trade. They were in one devil of a fix. He hated the thought of grubby hands on that lovely young woman.

Ethan was grim. "You see who it was?"

"No, but you gotta do somethin'," Billy said.

"Is Maggie all right?" Ethan asked as he sat up.

"Yeah."

"We got to get her back," Tyler said.

Paxton frowned. "They'll be bringing her to trade."

"We can't wait."

"If you go after her, you could both get killed," Ethan told him.

"I'm going!" Tyler leaped up and checked his sixgun.

"Your father's right," Paxton said. "And she won't be hurt as long as we got Slap."

Tyler turned slowly to look at Ethan. "Well, Pa?"

"They'll be waitin' for you, son."

Suddenly, something struck the front door with a loud bang. Paxton turned the lamps down and out. A pale light came from the fire in the iron stove.

Tyler slid the board cover aside and peered through the curtains. He could see a figure in the moonlight on the far boardwalk. It was a man he didn't recognize.

"I wanta talk!" the man shouted.

Ethan reached for his six-gun and checked the load. He was still hurting bad, but this was *his* fight. Tyler swallowed hard and waited as the man crossed the muddy street and came near the window.

"What do you want?" Tyler called.

"I got a message for you from Hop Dooley. He'll trade the girl for his brother."

Tyler's mouth was so dry it hurt. He looked at his father, who shook his head. Painfully, Tyler shouted back:

"We got to talk about it."

"Have Slap at the bridge in one hour or the girl's gonna disappear."

"One hour," Tyler said.

And the man hurried up the boardwalk toward the bridge.

Tyler slid the window cover in place and turned as Paxton brought the lamplight back to bright. He could feel needles in his gut as he gazed at his father, who was resting on his elbow.

"I got to try," Tyler said.

"All right, son," Ethan responded, looking worried. "But you could get shot down. You don't even know where she is."

"I'll go with him," Paxton offered.

"No," Tyler said. "You stay here with my father. They might be hoping we'd leave to go after her."

"I'll go," Billy said. "I could pound on the front door and make a lot of noise, and you could get 'em from the back. They'd never suspect me."

Tyler shook his head. "No, Billy. But you can show me what happened to Celia."

After a long glance at his father, Tyler left with the boy, both carrying rifles. In case they were being watched, they headed back toward the Rollins yard, cut through it, and circled back behind the buildings toward the livery.

"I didn't see 'em cross the bridge," Billy whispered. "The water's pretty high, so they had to cross, maybe while you were in the jail. On the other hand, it could be a trap to get us out in the open. In that case, you'd better get back to Maggie's."

"But where is Celia if they didn't take her across?"

"Only one place. The livery."

"It's got a big loft. You think she's up there?"

"I'll find out soon enough."

Billy insisted on helping, and he went around the front of the livery while Tyler slipped through the back corrals.

The front doors to the barn were partly open, and a lantern was burning near the small office, as usual. It cast an eerie glow across the open expanse of straw and gear and bunks, and threw shadows of boards and poles inside the stalls lining the wall to his left and farther down to his right.

It looked as if someone had been sleeping on the first bunk and then had left in a hurry. There was no sign of anyone, and the only sound was of a nervous horse. Toward the back, a long, spindly ladder led to the loft. The back entrance was open to the corrals.

Billy stood alone at the entrance. After a deep breath, he called out, "Mr. Paxton?" Then he walked farther inside, his rifle balanced in his hands. He prayed all eyes were on him, because he could see Tyler moving through the corral just outside.

As Billy kept calling out for Paxton, Tyler got to the back of the barn, where he saw an outside, heavy rope dangling from a beam up above at the big window to the loft. If it could haul bundles of hay, it should hold him, he figured.

Sticking his rifle through his belt, he began to climb hand over hand, the harsh rope tearing at his skin. He didn't dare bounce against the wall. Above, the beam groaned and creaked. He made an easy target, climbing in the open air. He could still hear Billy walking around and calling for Paxton. As he neared the beam, he heard a snarl from the loft:

"Hey, kid, get out of here. You're keepin' us awake."

"Mr. Paxton up there?" Billy called.

"No, he ain't. Now get out of here."

Tyler didn't recognize the voice. It could be a drifter, and Celia might really be over on the other side. Chilled through, he reached the beam and with great effort swung his legs over it. Then he inched toward the window.

As he drew himself up onto the beam, he looked inside. Two men were leaning over the edge of the loft next to the ladder. Something was rolled up in the straw behind them.

"Mr. Paxton coming back?" Billy shouted.

"You get outta here or I'm comin' down and whup you."

"All right," Billy said. "You don't have to get mad."

Tyler crawled along the beam and onto the straw, landing

on his knees with his rifle aimed. The two men, outlined in the pale light with six-guns in hand, heard the sound and spun about.

"Hands up!" Tyler ordered.

As the men opened fire, Tyler pulled the trigger on his Winchester. One bullet went through his hat, another missed.

Tyler's first shot hit one man in the chest, and he went sailing over backward. The other man was still firing, and Tyler shot again, this time hitting him square between the eyes. The man twisted and rolled off the loft.

Tyler leaped to his feet and ran to the bundle in the straw. He knelt quickly and pulled the blankets apart.

But it wasn't Celia. It was an old drifter they had killed to keep the barn silent.

"Tyler," Billy called. "You all right?"

Grumbling to himself, Tyler went to the ladder and hurried down to where the two men lay on their backs, staring up, their life gone.

"They work for Crocker," Billy said. "I seen 'em drivin' the wagons. One of 'em is Charlie. The big one, that's Hank."

"Celia's not here. She must be on the other side. I figure these two were going to back shoot us after the trade. Right now, I'm going across—alone."

"You only got a half hour, and they'll see you crossing the bridge. And they already heard the shootin'."

"I'll take my horse and swim across it, downstream."

"I don't like it, Tyler. That water's pretty rough about now. And deep. Ain't no horse ever swum it before."

"Just do as I say. You done good here, Billy. I'm right proud of you. But I got to go."

"They'll be watchin' for you."

"Go on, get over to the jail and tell them. Then get Maggie over to Filer's."

Tyler went for his black, his good swimming horse. He threw on a bridle and jumped on bareback, rifle in hand. Then he rode out through the back corrals in the pale moonlight. At the raging creek, he set his black into the water. The current caught them and tossed them about, but the sturdy animal kept swimming.

On the other side, Tyler rode his black out through the flooded area and toward the back of the east side of the wild part of town.

There were shacks and tents spread out behind the buildings. He could see Crocker's corrals farther north.

He reined up, wondering where Celia might be. They wouldn't be so obvious as to have her at Crocker's freight office, and they'd want to be close to the bridge. It had to be the first saloon, where he saw a pale light in the back window.

Sliding from the black, Tyler knew he was taking a wild chance. He left the animal ground-tied and moved slowly toward the back door. The window was too high to see inside, but he figured they were all in there. He tried the back door handle, but it was latched inside.

He started pounding on the door.

"Who is it?" a man yelled.

Tyler drew his bandanna over his mouth and shouted, "It's Charlie. Open up. They got Hank."

He heard cussing inside and a heavy wooden bar being moved. The door opened wide to a storeroom, and a small man was standing there, his back to the light, his hat lopsided on his head of curly hair.

Tyler shoved his rifle deep in the man's gut.

"Move."

"Hey, it's the law."

Tyler marched the man backward, and he could see another, bigger man with a black mustache rising from a chair. Bound and gagged, Celia was sitting on a box against the wall. There was no sign of Hop or Crocker.

"Untie her or I blow his guts out," Tyler said.

But the other man drew his six-gun. "I ain't facin' Hop over this," he snarled.

Tyler shoved his rifle so hard into the curly-haired man's gut that the fellow turned blue. Then he shoved him aside.

At the same time, Tyler drew his Colt and both men fired. The big man staggered backward, a bullet in his chest, his eyes crazed as he grabbed at air. He dropped his six-gun and clutched his wound. He dropped to his knees and fell face-down.

The curly-haired man was doubled up and groaning on the floor. Any minute, others would come running.

Tyler ran to Celia and pulled the gag from her mouth. He pulled a knife from the dead man's belt and slashed her bonds. She gave a cry of relief, but when she tried to stand, her legs gave way.

They could hear boots running on the boardwalk.

Tyler threw her over his left shoulder, his arm around her legs, and then he turned and raced for the back door. Out in the dark, he placed her on the black and then leaped up behind her.

They heard shouting as he set the black into a sudden gallop. As they reached the creek, a bullet whistled by his head. Then another. He knew what he had to do, and he reined up short at the bank. He slid off and shoved the reins in her hand. Then he hit the black on the rump.

"Get to the jail."

"No, Tyler!" she cried.

But he stayed behind while the horse started swimming across the heavy current, carried downstream but steadily fighting toward the far bank. Celia held on to the thick mane for dear life. Tyler dropped to one knee. There was no cover. He could hear swearing and muffled argument.

"I ain't goin' out there," a man shouted.

Tyler glanced back to see that Celia had made it across, then he started moving up the creek toward the bridge. It was a couple of hundred yards ahead. He held his rifle ready.

Instinctively he turned, and saw five men running out of the back of the saloon. Moonlight danced on his rifle, and they saw him and opened fire.

Bullets whistling around him, Tyler fired back and hit one man. But now they were taking cover and he had none. Four men were rapidly throwing lead his way, and he would be hit any second. He turned and dived into the raging creek.

"Blast!" Hop shouted. "Don't let him get away!"

Tyler went sailing down with the current, fighting to hold on to his rifle and make his way to the south bank. A chunk of wood struck him in the middle of the back, stunning him. He went under, losing his hat and rifle.

Fighting his way to the surface, he gasped for air. One man was already running down the bank and firing at him. Tyler went under again, the water his only chance. The raging current threw him about and carried him downstream until he crashed

109

into something. He realized it was a wheel from the wagon he had seen in the creek when he first came to town. Nearly frozen, he grabbed on tight and raised himself high enough to breathe. He prayed that the moon wouldn't reflect on his face as he fought for air.

Hanging on to the wagon in the raging creek, Tyler could see the far bank, where a dozen men were running about in the moonlight. Rifles gleamed in the pale glow. Six-guns were drawn, and big, fat Hop was frantically running up and down the bank like a prowling grizzly.

"There's his hat!" a man shouted above the roar of the water.

"Don't let him get away!" Hop bellowed.

"He's drowned by now," another yelled. "He never came up on the other bank, or I'd have seen 'im. He's dead, Hop."

But Hop wasn't so sure, and he hollered at them to go up and down the bank just the same. Tyler held on, watching half the men head downstream and the rest go toward the bridge. He was soaked through and nearly frozen.

"Nobody could swim in that," a man shouted.

Tyler turned to look toward the south bank and saw a figure kneeling near the barn. Someone had come to help, but whoever it was would figure, just like Dooley, that he had drowned.

It seemed hours before the men gave up and headed back toward the back door of the saloon. But Hop kept looking back at the creek. Finally, they all disappeared inside. And there was no longer a watching figure by the livery barn.

Tyler had no body heat left, his skin was like ice, and his heart was nearly at a stop. His body was hunched against the wagon wheel, and the south bank was at least ten feet away.

He didn't believe he could make it, but he had to try. He

moved to the side of the wagon, turned, and braced his feet against it. Then he lunged forward. The current caught him up like a toy, tossing him as he fought to swim across. He went under again and was thrown about crazily.

Another chunk of wood hurtled toward him and bounced off his arm. He was spun around, and went under again. This time he nearly drowned. He clawed at the surface and tried to swim.

His arms were like chunks of ice, and could barely slap the water. He prayed and fought, but he kept going under. He was continually struck and dipped and thrown, and yet he struggled on.

Suddenly, he was slammed against the south bank. He grabbed at the rocks on the edge. He frantically caught at a clump of brush, and he pulled himself against the bank. But he was so cold that he didn't think he could even pull himself up.

It was hopeless, and yet he held on and fought.

And there was a hand closing down on his. Tyler caught his breath and looked up in the moonlight to see his father kneeling, still weak and hurting and bandaged under his leather coat, but out here looking for his son.

Just seeing Ethan gave him tremendous strength, and Tyler pulled himself up out of the water with his father's help, and then he rolled over on the bank. As Tyler sat up, Ethan pulled off his coat and threw it around him.

"Get up, son, or you'll freeze to death."

A voice called to them: "Ethan, if you don't get back to the jail, Maggie's going to eat me alive. Come on."

It was Paxton, striding toward them. Then he stopped and stared. "My gosh, he's alive! Tyler's alive!" Paxton knelt, put an arm around Tyler, and dragged him to his feet. "I'll be! I saw you go under, but Ethan said you'd make it. I figured you was dead."

"He will be," Ethan growled, "if you don't stop talkin' and get him back to the jail."

Paxton half carried Tyler while Ethan walked at his son's side. They passed the livery, then made it across the street and up to the jail. Paxton reached out and pounded. "Open up. We're back."

The door swung open and Maggie stood there, frantic. "Oh, Ethan, I was so worried." Then she caught her breath. "Tyler!"

As he was dragged inside, Tyler saw Celia rising from his bunk, a blanket around her. Shining hair spilled about her pretty face and throat, and her eyes were round with surprise.

Tyler was dragged over to his bunk as the door was being barred, and Paxton laid him down. Maggie helped the weak Ethan to his bunk, and then she leaned over Tyler.

"Get his clothes off," she ordered. "Fast."

"You got to leave," Tyler moaned.

"Hush up, young man. We won't be looking." Paxton started to peel off Tyler's clothes and boots. Too frozen to feel anything, Tyler could barely sense the rough blankets being wrapped around his body. Paxton then rolled him over on the bunk and started to massage and pound him.

Celia came over. "Let me help."

Tyler tried to look up, but Paxton kept beating on him.

Billy was at her side. "Is he gonna die?"

"No," Celia said. "I'm beginning to think you just can't kill a Mandell or a Sinclair."

Maggie took Billy away, and Tyler was coughing up water as Paxton continued to pound his body and massage him with fierce hands. Before long, warmth began to return to Tyler's skin and he was able to roll over and sip the hot coffee Paxton offered him.

Lying on his side, Tyler looked at Celia, who had knelt at his side with Maggie. And he saw Billy with Paxton, who was resting at the desk. Across the room, a weary Ethan was lying on his bunk and looking relieved.

Tyler realized he had no clothes under his blankets, and his face turned beet-red. Maggie's hand was on his brow.

"Much better," she said, rising. "Now you need some hot food."

"And you women need to get out of here," Tyler muttered. "They mean business."

"The judge will be here tomorrow," Maggie told him.

"Too late," Tyler moaned. He drew a deep breath, then looked up again, and there was Celia, close to him, her hand on his exposed arm.

"That was a brave thing you did," she said softly. She touched his hot brow with her cool fingers.

"Come, Celia," Maggie said. "Let him sleep."

As Celia hesitated, Tyler told her, "You women and Billy got to get out of here. Hop would like nothin' better than to get rid of every one of us at the same time."

Maggie, standing nearby, drew herself up. "We can shoot just as well as you, Tyler Sinclair."

"Tyler's right," Ethan said. "Paxton, you take the women and Billy over to Filer's. But watch yourself."

Celia rose slowly and walked with Maggie to the door.

"I wanta stay," Billy insisted.

"The women need you," Ethan said.

And soon they were all gone but Ethan. Tyler got up with a great effort and barred the door. Then he sat down again.

"Get dressed, son. You'll feel better."

Tyler was still cold, but he could feel his strength returning. He gazed at his father, wanting to kiss him even with the big handlebar mustache. But he just smiled as he spoke.

"You sure looked mighty pretty down by the creek."

"So did you," Ethan said with a grin.

"You know, Hop's going to come at us with everything he's got. And this time, maybe Crocker will be right there with him."

"Well, it's a fact that Crocker would sure like to see the law dead and buried around here."

Tyler found his dry clothes and dressed, but his boots were still soaked through. He put them next to the iron stove, worried that they would shrink up on him.

After telling Ethan what had happened after Celia went into the creek, he poured them both some coffee. Ethan sat up on his bunk, and Tyler sat near him, marveling at the man's recovery.

"This jail ain't no fortress," Tyler said. "That door would come down easy."

"I know that, son. Sometimes, I think Filer planned it that way when he built this place. It sure wasn't put together like something he wanted around for a long time."

"So you think Filer wants to own everything, just like Crocker."

"He does, and that's a fact. Crocker borrowed heavy from Filer's bank, and sooner or later, Filer's gonna get that freight contract. I figure that Filer was hoping to marry Maggie and get her business. Then he'd control the freight charges up to the pass and get rich."

Ethan lay back on his bunk and closed his eyes. Paxton returned, stretched out on Tyler's, and was soon snoring.

After checking that his harmonica was still in his vest pocket, Tyler tapped water out of it, then got up and began to pace about. Somewhere out there in the night, Crocker and his boys were getting ready for something. He walked into the back of the jail.

Slap was sitting on his bunk. "What do you want?" he snarled.

"Just wanted to see if you were resting up for your trial."

"Nobody's going to hang me."

"Maybe they'll let you off with life in prison over at Canon City. How'd you like that?"

"My brothers and Crocker will get me out. You wait and see."

"They tried tonight. Grabbed Miss Rollins to trade, but they didn't get away with it."

Slap's eyes narrowed. "Get out of here! I don't want you around."

"Now, the judge might go easy on you if you was to help us out."

"Like how?"

"Tell us who killed the Rollins men."

"I don't know nothin' about that."

Tyler grimaced. "And who paid you and Jump to come after me."

"I ain't got nothin' more to say. So get out of here." Tyler left him, closing the door on the cells. He went back to the stove and shoved in more wood. Then he sat down at the desk, put his feet up, and took out his harmonica. As he played softly, he thought of Celia. He had sure gotten riled up when she was taken prisoner by Hop Dooley.

Hours passed, and he slept a little in the chair. When he heard something strike the front door, he jumped to his feet, hand on his holster. Maybe it was a trick to get him close to the front.

And then the deafening explosion knocked him back against the desk as the front wall crumbled and the roof came hurtling down. Boards and windows heaped upon them, and he was knocked to his knees, but he came up, shaking his head and pulling his Colt.

The echo of the explosion was still rumbling. He saw no one in the dark street, and the office lamp was on the floor, spilling oil, but the flame was out. He hurried over to Ethan, who was pulling himself out of the mess.

Paxton was crawling out of the boards and coming over to them. "Get in back," Ethan mumbled.

"No, you and Paxton go ahead, and I'll watch here."

"Son, that was dynamite."

"But they won't take a chance on hurting Slap."

"He's right," Paxton said. "Look, they may rush us. I'll stay out here. We got plenty of cover."

Ethan was uncertain. "Then I'll stay out here."

"Someone's got to be with Slap," Tyler said, "and you're in bad shape. You can't do no running out here."

Reluctantly, Ethan put a weak hand on his son's shoulder and went into the back room. But Tyler was worried, and he knelt near Paxton.

"I don't like that back door out there," he whispered.

"It's a heavy door and well barred."

"Get down. They're moving in."

Both men dropped down behind portions of fallen roof, silent as they watched figures approaching from all directions. Men were moving along the boardwalks, behind the buildings, in alleys.

"I count fifteen," Tyler murmured.

Paxton, rifle ready, peered around them. "Maybe more."

And the sudden rush of violent gunfire exploded in the stillness, bullets flying through the wood and pounding the walls behind them. They ducked low and held their fire, even as men came rushing onto the boardwalk.

They waited until seven men were stumbling over the debris, and then they opened fire with six-guns and rifles. The noise was so loud it covered the cries of the dying men.

Suddenly Hop was charging across the boards, knocking everything down as he rushed at Tyler, who was firing and hitting but not stopping the man.

More men charged, and Paxton was firing at them, but Tyler was crushed by the furious body of Hop Dooley, who was pounding him down even as Hop's blood spilled all over them.

Tyler slammed his fist in the man's face, and Hop rolled over. He shoved away the dying man while Paxton kept firing, and then he heard a crash in the back. He jumped to his feet and opened the door to find Ethan trying to block a battering ram.

The back door crashed open and four men spilled inside. Tyler fired, hitting the first man, and Ethan got the next two. Tyler got the fourth man, who screeched as he fell.

Tyler shoved the broken door closed and put the bar in

place, made sure Ethan was okay, and then stumbled back up front to where Hop was still alive and mumbling. He knelt by the big man.

"You're dying, Hop, so you'd better make peace with the Lord. Did you kill the Rollins men?"

Glassy-eyed, Hop shook his head. "No."

"Crocker didn't hire it done?"

Hop again shook his head, even as Ethan came to stand close to where Tyler was kneeling. Hop was grabbing at his bleeding chest, eyes round and vacant. Tyler was persistent:

"Did Crocker pay Jump and Slap to kill me?"

"Yeah," the man murmured, closing his eyes. "And also the girl."

"And Crocker paid Smithers to kill the marshal?"

"Yeah."

"And did he hire this jailbreak?"

"Yeah."

"And did he pay you and your brothers to stop the Rollins wagons?"

Hop nodded and then gasped in pain.

"Hold on. The doctor's on his way," Tyler said.

"When Skip gets back," Hop mumbled, "you're a dead man."

Tyler stood up slowly and glanced at Ethan, but before he could speak, Hop gave a spasm and died. The fighting had stopped. Smoke and dust still rose from the broken wall. The moonlight was bright now, dust rising into its glow.

"Hop was right, son. Skip is a dangerous man. You're goin' to have to watch yourself."

And Slap was still in his cell, grabbing the bars with a frantic look on his face, sweat on his nose and brow.

Tyler made more repairs to the back door. Paxton came inside and reported that, including Hop, seventeen men had died. The sun was slowly casting its light on the street as Paxton started to close the front door.

Peter Filer was striding up the boardwalk, and other people were peering out their windows up and down the street.

"I come to find out what was happening," he said.

"Hop Dooley is dead," Paxton told him.

Peter could barely contain his joy. "Oh, that's too bad."

Tyler ordered some men to haul the bodies over to the undertaker. As the street and jail area became clear of the dead, he began to relax.

Peter looked the lawmen over. "It should be an interesting trial. Right now, I have to go tell Mrs. Rollins and her daughter that everything's all right. My father's trying to keep them inside." He strolled away with his head held high, as if he owned the town and Celia Rollins.

"Look," Paxton said.

Coming across the bridge were four men and a buggy with an important-looking driver. It was the judge, a wiry, hard-faced man, and Tyler went to meet him.

"Judge, we got Slap Dooley in jail. But we got one more criminal to bring over—Wiley Crocker."

"We'll hold court at one o'clock. That enough time?"

Tyler nodded, then stepped back as the buggy and the riders moved on. Troubled, he went back to where Ethan was sitting in a chair Paxton had rescued.

"Pa, if Crocker didn't have the Rollins men killed, who did?"

"He could have done it without telling Hop. Right now,

we'll get Crocker for conspiracy to commit murder and as an accessory. Let's go."

"You ain't fit," Tyler said.

"I've been in worse shape than this and killed three men at the same time and kept my prisoner."

Tyler grinned. "Yeah, I read about it. But me and Paxton will take Crocker easy."

And so it was that Tyler and Paxton crossed over to the north side.

"Crocker got more men over here?" Tyler asked. "Maybe, but a lot of 'em are just freighters. Most of his gunmen are dead now. But he's an arrogant man. He won't figure we know he's involved."

When they reached the freight office, the door was open, and Crocker sat puffing on his pipe, looking innocent and a little annoyed.

"Deputy, can't you see I'm busy?"

"Didn't you hear the shooting?"

"Yeah, I heard about it. Slap has a lot of friends." Tyler was grim. "And they all work for you."

"So what? I didn't know they were goin' to be fool enough to try to bust Slap out of jail."

"Hop Dooley was killed. But before he died, he said you paid Slap and Jump to kill me, and you also paid for the jailbreak."

"That's a lie!" Crocker roared.

"You're under arrest."

Crocker jumped to his feet and reached for the Sharps on the wall, but the two deputies seized him, jerked him around, and cuffed his hands behind his back.

"You can't get away with this," Crocker snarled.

But they took him into custody and threw him into the cell next to Slap, who stared at him with his mouth wide-open.

"Mr. Crocker, I didn't tell 'em nothin'."

"Shut up!" Crocker snarled.

Soon after, the prisoners were marched to trial.

Court was held in the hotel dining room, with chairs set up and everyone in town crowded in for a view. Acting as if he'd never been shot, Ethan was the prosecutor, and Percy Filer was representing the prisoners, all seated at tables in front of the rows of chairs. The twelve men chosen as jurors, most of them merchants, were seated to the far right wall.

Crocker was charged with conspiring to murder Tyler, and with conspiring to commit a jailbreak. Slap was charged with the attempted murder of Tyler and the murder of his brother. Because the evidence would be duplicated, the men were tried together.

"Wait till Skip gets back," Slap hollered as he was plunked down in the front row next to the Filers. "He'll kill anyone who says anything against me."

The small but angry judge pounded his gavel on the desk he was using, and he glared around the room, his thin face twisted. As silence fell, he leaned back and said, "Proceed, Mr. Prosecutor."

Ethan, his wounds hurting, remained seated behind a small table next to Tyler, who was his first witness. Tyler testified about the incident at the cabin that led to Jump's murder, and he reported Hop's dying accusations against Crocker. Then Celia and Billy were called to testify.

After hearing the witnesses, the jury did not even have to leave the room. They had a brief huddle, and then the foreman said, "Guilty as charged, Your Honor."

Slap was frantic and yelling and had to be subdued. Crocker looked pale and stricken, and then wild with anger.

"Slap Dooley," the judge said, "you are sentenced to life in prison. Wiley Crocker, twenty years."

The prisoners were taken away by Paxton and two other men. Slap's shrieks and threats continued outside. Percy Filer exchanged a grin with his son. They knew they would soon take over Crocker's holdings.

With the prisoners on their way to Canon City under armed escort, the judge decided to stay over for the Fourth of July, which was the next day. The town slowly turned to plans for merrymaking. But at any moment. Skip Dooley could ride in to avenge his brothers. And Skip was the fast gun whom even his brothers had feared.

The lawmen went back to the jail, where men had already cleared off most of the debris and carried away the wall and roof. The back half of the jailhouse was still intact. Ethan sat down at his desk and dusted it with his hand. The sunlight shone on his silver-red hair.

Wearing a brand-new Stetson, Tyler pulled up a chair. "We still don't know who killed the Rollins men. Maybe it was Skip Dooley. He's the only one we ain't been talking to."

"He's pretty fast, I'll allow him that, and he could kill a man with pleasure. I reckon he'd have no trouble back shooting, either. Right now, we got to think about the holiday tomorrow. Everyone in tarnation is coming to town, even from the mines. We'll have to be on our toes, son."

"You're looking better."

"I'm used to being shot up. I got more holes in me than a beehive."

"But we'll put all that behind us, right, Pa?"

Ethan nodded, and Tyler suddenly felt weary and tired, exhausted from the short time he had been in Sweetwater. He thought of the men he had killed and of his confusion about Celia. But over it all, the thrill of finding and knowing his father was like a tonic.

"So this is what you've been doing."

The voice startled Tyler, and he slowly stood up, his mind clicking. He turned and stared with delight at Shorty. The small, pinch-faced cowpuncher, his hat pushed back from his damp forehead, dirty and unkempt, was standing on the boardwalk and grinning.

Tyler hurried to grab Shorty's hand. "Boy, am I glad to see you. Hey, Pa, this is my friend Shorty from the Hawkens ranch."

Ethan reached up to shake the visitor's hand as Tyler led him over. "Glad to meet you."

Shorty was open-mouthed. "So Mandell really is your Pa?"

"Sure is. And what brings you here? I ain't going back to the ranch, you know. Pa and me, we got things to do."

"That ain't why I came, Tyler. I brung you a letter."

EIGHT

*S*horty reached inside his vest pocket and drew out a damp, crumpled envelope. "It came from that Sinclair fellow in Kentucky."

Tyler took it, his mouth dry. "Uh, sure. Look, Shorty, you go get yourself some chuck at the hotel. Pa and me, we'll be along shortly."

Left alone with his father, Tyler took out the letter and read it aloud:

"Dear Mr. Sinclair: We regret to inform you that Walden Sinclair, your stepfather, died last winter when he was shot by a dissatisfied client in front of his office. The man was executed. In his will, Mr. Sinclair left all his property to his brother except for a bequest to you of five thousand dollars, provided you could be located within five years.

"Now that you have been found, it is important that you contact a local attorney or a bank officer to arrange for the legal transfer of this gift."

The letter was signed by a lawyer he didn't know. Tyler stared at it feeling a strange sense of redemption. His stepfather had not really disliked him after all. The man had thought enough of him to leave him a legacy, something to give him a new start in life, perhaps to make up for what had been missing, for the way he had been scorned by both families.

Drawing a deep breath, Tyler handed the letter to his father. "I can't believe it. I thought he never cared much about me."

"He was enough of a man to make things right, son."

"I guess this means we got money to do whatever we want, Pa. And I got a real hankering for Montana."

Ethan grinned. "Whatever you say. We'll clean things up here and make our plans. But tomorrow, I got to do some sparking."

Tyler folded the letter and put it into his pocket. "Let's hope Skip Dooley doesn't spoil the party."

"What about you and Celia?"

"I don't know, Pa. I don't think she really likes me. And I got this problem with women."

"Look at me, son. Are you afraid of Celia Rollins?"

Tyler flushed with color. "Maybe I've been hiding behind what Ma done, and that girl in Texas. Because of them. I'm afraid to take a chance."

"That sounds like a man talking."

Tyler grinned, pleased. It seemed that everything his father said to him gave him pleasure. But it also gave him deep regret that he had missed all his young years with this man.

"Now you listen, Pa. If Skip Dooley comes riding in, you leave him to me. I don't want nothing happening to you. And besides, I'm a heck of a lot faster."

"We'll talk about that later. Now let's go find your friend."

After a good meal at the hotel with Shorty, who had some

funny stories to tell about Tyler, the three men checked into the hotel.

They each had a hot bath, then retired to their room and talked long into the night. By morning, they had had only a few hours of sleep. They shaved and dressed, and peered out the window at the folks already setting up tables and banners.

"I sure want to win that One in a Thousand Winchester," Tyler said. "They're supposed to be the finest rifles made."

Ethan grinned. "Celia thinks *she's* going to win it."

"A woman?" Shorty grunted.

"She's won every year," Ethan said.

Before noon they were moving down among the happy crowd: grizzled miners who smelled plenty, cowhands with wages in their pockets, suspicious characters from the north side, prettied-up women spreading tables of fancy food and sparkling punch, merchants plying their wares. A rickety band played patriotic music that carefully avoided any songs from the War Between the States. Children and dogs ran about.

Ethan and Tyler were in charge, and everyone felt safe for the first time in years. The Filers were sporting black broadcloth coats and vests, linen shirts, black silk cravats, and paper collars. They were always around Maggie and Celia. Ethan was still weak and had to do a lot of sitting, but Tyler kept an eye on things. There was some mention of Skip Dooley, but everyone wanted to forget about him.

Wearing a pretty green dress with a velvet jacket, Maggie was dishing out punch and flirting shamelessly with Ethan, who was sitting nearby and whose face was always red. Billy was running around with other boys, and the little puppy followed him, its ears flopping as it barked at firecrackers.

And at the end of the street behind the livery, a long panel was being set up as a shooting range against a series of earth piles, each with targets. A large banner proclaimed the prize as the special edition of a One in a Thousand Winchester repeater. Everyone passed by to gaze at the shining weapon with the engraved markings.

Tyler found himself looking for Celia. He saw her once, surrounded by young cowhands who were carrying her things. Uneasy, he turned away. He ate some of the fantastic food on the tables, appreciating what great cooks these frontier women really were.

At the contest, he was standing in line with his rifle when he felt someone standing rather close.

Turning, he saw Celia gazing up at him in the sunlight, her hair like spun gold. She was wearing green and lace, and she looked so pretty that he had to swallow. In her small hands was a Winchester repeater. She looked different, more feminine, but there was something he couldn't read shining in her eyes. "Well, Tyler Sinclair, I guess you're quite a hero."

He was embarrassed. "I don't know about that."

"You brought in Slap Dooley and Crocker. And you rescued me twice."

"But you still don't like me."

She didn't answer, just gave him a mysterious little smile.

He frowned, looking her over, wishing he could understand her, wondering how he could steal another kiss. She sure hadn't pushed him away.

The contest was announced, and even Shorty was in line. Ethan, however, just sat in the sun and watched, with Maggie at his side and fussing over him. The Filers came to stand near Maggie, with Percy trying to get her attention.

Tyler's competition was intense. Many fine shots, including Shorty, hit the distant targets over and over, but when it came to closing in the shots, Tyler was in the lead. Celia came to take her turn. She matched Tyler shot for shot, and he wondered how a man could live with a woman if she could out-shoot him.

And then it was down to him and Celia.

They matched each other, again and again.

Finally, the judges threw up their hands. "It's a tie. And only one rifle. So now what?"

Tyler swallowed. "Let her have it."

"No," Celia said. "We'll share it."

But the judge wouldn't approve. "I'll toss a coin, a silver dollar. See if you can hit that."

The coin went sailing into the air before Tyler could work another shell into his rifle, so he drew his sixgun and fired, his hand moving so fast it was a blur. The bullet struck the silver dollar, spinning it and knocking it down. There was a hole clean through the center.

The crowd was stunned, but the judge shook his head. "This is a rifle match, young fellow. You got to do it with a rifle. Let's hope you ain't used up your luck."

Once again the judge tossed a silver dollar. The coin sailed toward the sky, reflecting the sunlight. This time Tyler was ready with his rifle, and he fired fast. The bullet hit the dollar and spun it again. When it fell, there was a hole right through the middle, as before. The judge picked it up, staring in disbelief, and the crowd cheered.

Celia wet her lips as she worked a shell into her Winchester. A silver dollar flew into the air, high and shining. She fired.

And she missed. The judge said she ought to have another chance because Tyler had had two shots. No one protested. She fired again. And again she missed.

The judge picked up the One in a Thousand Winchester. He ran his fingers lovingly along the perfect lines. Then he handed it to Tyler, who took it in both hands.

Ever since he had first heard about these perfect rifles, Tyler had wanted one. Now it was here, cold and beautiful in his grip. He looked at Celia, expecting envy, but seeing only a real sportsman's smile.

He turned to see his father's proud grin, and then he walked over and handed him the rifle. "Take care of this, will you, Pa?"

"Time to dance!" someone shouted. "Let's go! Over to the hotel, out back in the garden!"

It was then that Peter Filer stepped in and said, "Come along, Celia. I know all the latest steps."

She glanced at Tyler, then took Peter's arm and walked with him into the happy crowd.

Feeling helpless, Tyler turned to his father, who was still with Maggie and Percy. "I can't dance," Tyler said.

Maggie smiled. "I'll teach you."

Ethan got to his feet, and Maggie and Tyler walked with him, Percy still crowding them. They headed for the dance. Ethan was parked on a bench, and Maggie took the rifle from Tyler and handed it to Ethan.

"Do you mind, Ethan?" she asked.

"No, I'll wait my turn."

Percy was bristling. "Maggie, isn't this our dance?"

"Now, Percy, you can wait. Tyler here has got to learn a few steps."

As Maggie led Tyler onto the dance floor, Ethan looked from Tyler to the rifle in his hands. His son had a red face, but Ethan was mighty proud.

"I'd give my life for that boy."

Percy muttered something and turned away.

Tyler was soon doing a few quick steps with Maggie, who told him, "You see? Just follow the music. You don't really have to know anything."

"I know one thing."

She swayed in his arms as they turned. "What's that?"

"My father's a lucky man."

Maggie blushed. "So am I. A man like that with such a deep and wonderful soul. And a handsome son."

Tyler pressed her hand. If only she had been his mother all these years, he might have been a happier man.

The wild tune continued, and he looked over and saw Peter whirling about with Celia. When the music stopped, he was still watching her.

"Go ahead," Maggie said.

"She don't like me much."

"Be brave, Tyler."

He shrugged, and she pushed him toward Celia, who paused to stare at him. Peter had a possessive hold on her arm, but Tyler walked right up as the music started.

"Dance, Miss Celia?"

"She's busy," Peter said.

But Tyler took Celia's arm and pulled her away from Peter, who was furious and steaming. Celia didn't resist, and she slid into Tyler's embrace, her right hand in his left, his right arm encircling her. She was still staring at him as the music started.

It was a waltz. Tyler made some clumsy steps. He was in total distress, his face darkening, his mouth tight. He was embarrassed and felt foolish, and he stopped. Quickly, Peter appeared and grabbed Celia's hand. "Let a man who knows how to waltz handle this, Tyler."

Tyler moved out of the crowd and to the edge of the garden, his face burning. He glanced around to see Maggie and Ethan dancing gracefully. And Shorty was doing a high-step with a pretty young woman.

Tyler turned into the shade, around behind a giant tree near the hotel's back porch. He drew out his bandanna and wiped his brow. He had been a hero. Now he felt like a fool.

The music played long and sweet, and then it stopped.

"Tyler."

He turned to see Celia standing near him. She was alone, and she reached out to touch his arm.

"We didn't finish our dance," she said.

"I can't dance."

"I saw you doing fine with Mama. The waltz is just different, that's all. I could teach you easy."

"I ain't got time."

"Tyler, you're not the kind of man to give up so easy."

It was then that Peter found them. "Come on, Celia. It's a polka."

She kept looking at Tyler even as Peter pulled her back into the sunlight. Feeling rotten, Tyler went up onto the porch and into the hotel. From the window, he could see the crowd having great fun. Celia was swaying in Peter's arms. Maggie and Ethan were walking up the street.

And Tyler slammed his fist against the wall.

*   *   *

While Tyler steamed, Ethan and Maggie were walking along the boardwalk, enjoying the warm sunlight. He was leaning on her, and she liked it. Just then, Paxton came hurrying over.

"Where's Tyler, Marshal? Skip Dooley's on the north side, and he's on his way over here. Reckon he heard about his brothers, and he's bound and determined to kill Tyler right off. So where is he?"

"I don't know," Ethan lied. "Maggie, you go back. I'm going with Paxton."

She was frightened, and she squeezed his arm. "No, Ethan."

Standing numb and helpless, Maggie watched Paxton and the marshal walking up the street past the abandoned tables and debris.

*   *   *

Still angry at himself, Tyler was standing near the back door of the hotel. He turned and walked into the empty lobby and toward the front door.

"Tyler."

He paused, then turned to look at Celia. She was coming toward him, and he backed away a few steps. But she hurried right up to him and put a hand on his arm.

"Tyler, won't you dance with me? Right here?"

The music from the garden was drifting around them, and she was close, smelling like lilacs, her eyes wide and glistening. They were alone and it was intoxicating.

"I'll show you," she said.

132

She came against his side, her left hand on his shoulder, her right reaching for his left. But Tyler put his arms around her and lifted her off the floor.

He bent his head and crushed her to him. His lips found her velvet lips, and his head was spinning. There was a terrible ringing in his ears. She hesitated, then kissed him back, her hands tightening on his shoulders.

"Tyler," a man called. "You got to come. Skip Dooley's comin' over the bridge. And the marshal's gone to meet him."

Tyler spun Celia from his arms, a madness enveloping him. His father had gone to face a killer, a fast gun. He could hardly breathe, and he broke into a run around the hotel.

To lose his father now would be the biggest heartbreak of all.

NINE

A crowd was gathering ahead on both sides of the street near the bridge.

His father would be facing Skip Dooley alone.

Frantic, Tyler could hardly breathe. He ran up beside Paxton, who stopped him.

Standing on the wooden bridge was a man with a black hat banded with conchos. His legs were apart and his hands at his sides. He had a thick black mustache and long hair, and his boots had fancy red markings. He was a big man, thick in the chest but lean and limber at the waist. He wore two sidearms, hung low and tied down. Death was written all over him.

And facing him, his back to Tyler, was Ethan Mandell.

Tyler pushed away from Paxton, but he knew he was going to be too late. He staggered through the crowd and stopped, breathless, because it was already happening.

Ethan was trying to save his son, and the terrible realization was tearing at Tyler's aching heart.

"You, Marshal," Skip snarled. "If you're too scared, you can just drop your guns."

"What do you want here, Skip?"

"My brothers are dead because of you and some deputy you got, and I'm here to set things right."

"Drop your guns," Ethan said.

"First you, then your deputy."

"If you don't drop your gun belt, I'm comin' over there and takin' it myself."

Skip grinned. "I would sure enough enjoy that." Tyler caught his breath as Ethan started toward the man. He knew that Skip was not going to wait. He couldn't step in and shame his father, but he was going crazy.

Skip's eyes narrowed and his nostrils flared.

And Skip drew, as did Ethan, and Skip's bullet struck the lawman on the side of the head, spinning him around. Ethan fell on his side, tried to get up, and then doubled up and lay still. His hat rolled to the side.

Tyler fought his tears, his anger so hot his face was burning. Skip was standing there with his smoking gun. Ethan had not even pulled the trigger. The gunman was too fast, the fastest Tyler had ever seen.

But Tyler walked slowly into the street, suddenly so cold he felt nothing but revenge.

Skip Dooley saw the star gleaming in the sunlight, and he grinned with a fierce joy, slowly holstering his six-gun.

"Well, then, you must be that fancy deputy."

Tyler fought the urge to look down at his father, for this was the moment of truth. His speed had been mightily tested, but never in a showdown with a fast gun like Skip.

His body felt like a chunk of ice. His knees barely worked as he walked a few more steps to place himself square in the street.

To his left was the broken front of the jailhouse. On his right was the livery. In front of him was Skip Dooley, a man so cold and brutal he could kill without hesitation.

"All right, Deputy. It's your turn."

"You're under arrest, Dooley."

"It was a fair fight."

"You're gonna stand trial."

Dooley snickered. "You're a fool, Deputy, and when this is over, you'll be a dead one. But looky here, if you want to turn and run, I won't stop you. Everyone would sure get a laugh out of it, but you'd be alive."

There was no way Tyler could turn from this terrible contest, and he said, "Drop your gun belt, Dooley. Now."

Skip's eyes narrowed, and his nostrils flared.

And the man drew, fast and sure, but Tyler drew at the same time, his thumb on the hammer before his Colt left the holster, and he was firing even as Skip pulled the trigger.

Tyler's bullet hit the man in the right side of his chest, and Skip's spun harmlessly past Tyler's ear.

Skip Dooley was standing on his feet, blood on his chest, his eyes round and staring, his mouth open. He keeled over forward, to his knees, his six-gun buried in the dry mud.

It was a long moment before Tyler realized he was still alive. He had to look down at himself to be sure. Then his senses returned and he saw Paxton kneeling with the wounded Skip, who had rolled onto his back.

"Skip, talk to me," Paxton said.

Skip glared up at him, mouth twisting. He tried to reach for Paxton, but his hands were too weak, and his arms fell back as his gold watch dropped from under his shirt. Paxton picked it up.

"Looky here, Tyler. This watch got smashed clean through. Probably saved ole Skip's life."

Turning about, Tyler saw Maggie and Celia running up the street, and Billy coming from the boardwalk as the crowd began to move closer.

Tyler was still numb as he knelt by his father and turned him face upward. Blood was red and hot on the side of Ethan's head, but his eyes were opening with a flutter of heavy lids.

Tyler grabbed his arm. "Ethan, doggone it, can't you ever stop scarin' me?"

Ethan blinked. "What happened?"

Billy knelt. "Tyler beat Skip Dooley fair and square. Never saw anything like it."

Ethan slid his hand up to take Tyler's, and he tried to sit up. Tyler grabbed his arm and pulled him to a sitting position. Tyler wrapped his bandanna around Ethan's head, and Paxton retrieved his hat. Ethan leaned against his son, whose arm went around his shoulder.

The doctor came and checked Ethan, who had been merely stunned by the bullet. Then he went over to the wounded Skip. Maggie and Celia came hurrying to them, and Maggie was the first to kneel.

"Ethan Mandell, I swear. When we're married, there'll be no more of this."

Ethan scowled. "I ain't asked you yet."

"But you will, won't you?"

He managed a weak grin and nod, and she squeezed his hand. Tyler watched their obvious affection, and he got wearily to his feet. Badly shaken, he hardly felt Celia's hand on his arm.

The doctor stood up, holding the smashed watch, and he pulled out a part of the dangling back cover and raised it to the sunlight. He looked down at the bleeding, cursing man, then back at the watch. Finally he handed it to Maggie. "It's got your husband's name on the back," he said.

She was startled, and stood up to stare at it. "This was his, all right. It was taken when he was killed."

Tyler spun, his hand on his holster, and he glared down at Skip, who was trying to sit up, even as the doctor sought to cleanse the wound.

"All right, Skip. I'm locking you up."

He and Paxton pulled the man to his feet, and the doctor started complaining, but Skip was pulled over to the remains of the jail and shoved into a cell in the still standing back room. Paxton stood guard while the doctor finished his job.

And Tyler went back onto the street to help Maggie with Ethan. She was crying, her face pink, her voice shaken.

"That Skip Dooley killed my husband. Crocker must have paid him. But Skip was in Denver when Jody was killed. So who killed Jody?"

Tyler glanced at the silent, tearful Celia. He shrugged and helped Ethan down to the freight office where Maggie could look after him. Celia followed, and Billy came running over to join them.

Tyler went back into the fading sunlight, and Celia came to stand near him. He couldn't look at her just yet, afraid she'd see the terror lingering, the horrible fear that he might have lost his father. And he was afraid he'd see suspicion back in her eyes. Yet her voice was soft.

"Tyler, you could have been killed."

"I nearly lost my pa again. I'm gettin' him out of here. Let Paxton take over."

She started to speak, then paused, because Percy and Peter Filer were coming across the street. The banker's gray eyes were almost white and he looked nervous.

"That was a fearful gunfight. Did you kill Skip Dooley?"

"No, he's alive," Tyler said.

Percy swallowed. "I see."

"Celia," Peter said, "you shouldn't be watching men kill each other."

After some idle conversation, the Filers turned and went back to the hotel. Tyler stared after them curiously. When Celia went inside the freight office to see her mother and Ethan, Tyler followed. Billy was there, playing with his pup. Shorty joined them.

As Maggie fussed over Ethan's small wound, Tyler put his hand on his father's shoulder. "We got to see the judge, Pa. I got to know how to change my name back to Mandell."

Ethan grinned. "That's the best news I've heard all night."

"No," Shorty said. "The best is my being your foreman."

Billy shook his head. "Ain't so. The best is Maggie and Ethan are gonna adopt me."

But up in their hotel room, the Filers were loosening their collars and sweating profusely. Percy sat down on the bed.

"That blasted Skip. Now what?"

"He'll shoot his mouth off," Peter said. "We got to shut him up."

Percy nodded. "Tonight. After dark."

TEN

While Ethan, Tyler, and Shorty retired to their room at the hotel, Paxton was guarding Skip at the remainder of the jailhouse. It was a cold night with a half-moon.

And after midnight, the Filers slipped out of their room and down the stairs. Outside, they moved silently, their long gray coats covering their rifles. Their hats were pulled down tight, and their bandannas were ready for drawing up over their faces, just in case. They would have to do the job and get back to the hotel fast, returning through the back cellar door. Their plans were made, and they were ready.

The front of the jail was still down, but the office door to the back cells was closed. A light could be seen under it, and Percy drew up his rifle and knocked.

"Who's there?" Paxton called.

"Percy Filer."

"Kind of late, ain't it?"

"The marshal gave me somethin' to give you."

They could hear the bar sliding aside. Paxton was standing in the lamplight as he opened the door, his six-gun in hand. Percy shoved his rifle hard in Paxton's belly, knocking the wind out of him, and Pete grabbed his six-gun. As Paxton tried to rise up, they beat him down with their rifle butts until he lay in his blood on the floor.

"He's a goner," Pete said.

Then both men turned to look at Skip, who had stood up with glee. "I knew you'd come to get me out."

"No time to talk," Pete said. Hurrying to the back door, he removed the bar while Percy guarded the front door.

Percy dragged Paxton over to the cells. "It'll look like Skip had grabbed him and banged his head on the bars."

"We got money for you," Peter said, unlocking the cell and handing over an envelope. "Now get out of town and don't come back."

Skip opened it and looked at the money. "Hey, that's the most greenbacks I ever did see. Thanks."

"Yeah, but I told you to throw that watch away," Percy snarled. "Now look at the fix you're in."

"Hey, it was a fancy, eight-day watch and real gold. But don't worry, I got friends all over and places to go."

"Hurry," Peter said. "There's a horse up by the aspens. We put plenty of grub on it."

Skip took his gun belt from the rack and strapped it on. "There's one thing I got to know. It was me that got old man Rollins, and you paid me well. But who done in Jody while I was gone?"

Peter drew himself up a little. "It was me."

Skip stared at him. "I suspected that, but I sure never believed it. Fancy man like you."

"Now hurry!" Percy said.

Skip grinned, went out the back into the moonlight, and hurried up the hill toward the aspens. The Filers stepped into the night and raised their rifles.

When Skip gained the rise and realized there was no horse, he turned. The Filers opened fire, filling him with lead, the noise cracking loud in the night. Skip jerked, fell, and rolled partway down the hill. Then he lay still, arms outspread, gun still in his holster.

"Get the money—quick!" Percy said.

Peter ran up the hill, knelt, pulled the money out, and found it covered with blood. Regardless, he stuck it in the inside pocket of his long coat. Then he ran back down the hill just as townspeople stirred and came outside their doors.

Tyler was running from the hotel, six-gun in hand, frantic as he realized that something must have happened to Paxton. He ran around the jail, saw the Filers, then ran inside and stared at Paxton's bloody form in the lamplight. He hurried out back to where the Filers were standing with their rifles pointed down.

Ethan was coming around the jail now, and he joined them just as Percy wiped his brow.

"Me and Peter, we was just taking a walk, and we heard some noise. We come around the jail and saw old Skip running up the hill."

"You always take a walk with your rifles?" Ethan asked.

"Marshal," Percy said, "what with all the fighting that's been going on, we just felt better having 'em with us, that's all. And lucky we did."

"Where was Skip going without a horse?" Tyler asked.

Peter shrugged. "We don't know anything about that. You're the lawmen, so you figure it out. Come on. Pa, let's turn in."

"Just wait awhile," Tyler said, and he went back in to kneel by Paxton. He sprang to his feet as Shorty appeared at the back door. "He's alive! Get the doc! Quick!"

Shorty took off, and Tyler went back outside to see the Filers getting plenty nervous. Ethan stood watch while Tyler went up the hill to check Skip, who, though filled with lead, was still alive. Tyler came back down, carrying Skip's six-gun.

"He's not dead, but he oughta be."

Percy's face was running with sweat. "We got to go, Marshal. Peter and me, we're a little shaken up by this."

"Just stay put," Ethan ordered.

The doctor came running and he hurried inside to kneel by Paxton. Ethan went inside too while Tyler stayed with the Filers. A crowd had gathered. Several men lifted Skip and Paxton and carried them to the doctor's office. Shorty and one of the men agreed to stand guard over Skip.

Now the lawmen and Filers were alone in the moonlight.

Then Celia and Maggie came running up, wrapped in long coats and looking frightened. Celia was carrying a lantern.

Peter turned and said to her, "Everything's all right, Celia."

As an affront to Tyler, Peter put a comforting arm around her, causing her to nearly drop the lamp. She was pressed against his chest, and could feel something wet. Her nimble fingers drew out the envelope dripping with blood. She sprang back and threw the envelope to the ground.

Tyler picked it up and handed it to Ethan, who studied the blood and money in the light of Celia's lamp. Then Celia, holding the lamp in both hands, hurried over to Maggie.

"Now then," Ethan said to Peter, "do you always carry this much money around with you? And why is it bloody?"

Peter grimaced. "Well, it was like this, Marshal. We saw Paxton in there, and I touched him. I reckon that I next reached inside my coat for something to clean my hand."

"That so?" Ethan grunted. "I thought you said you was walking around the jail and saw Skip going up the hill."

"That's right, but we saw Paxton first," Peter insisted.

"Here's the way I see it," Tyler said. "You two paid Skip to kill Mr. Rollins, and you couldn't take a chance on him confessing it. So you broke him out and then done him in."

Percy shook his head a few times. "You think what you want. Me and Peter are going to bed."

"No," Ethan said. "You're coming into the jail to make a statement. Then we'll see."

Suddenly, the Filers started backing away, rifles at their hips. "You leave us be," Percy said. "We didn't do nothing an honest citizen wouldn't do."

It was then that Billy came running over. He grabbed Maggie's arm, looked at the Filers with frightened eyes, and turned to Ethan.

"Paxton's okay," the boy said.

"And Skip?"

Billy was nervous. "Talking up a storm. He killed Mr. Rollins all right, and the Filers paid him."

"That's a lie," Percy said. "He's makin' it up."

"And that ain't all," Billy went on. "It was Peter Filer who shot down Jody. He was braggin' to Skip."

Celia and Maggie caught their breath in surprise.

"Lies!" Peter snapped. "Skip's crazy, just tryin' to save himself."

"Maybe," Tyler said. "But it makes a lot of sense. The two of you wanted both freight contracts and the whole town, and you were after these women to help you get it."

"Worse," Ethan added, "you Filers gave that money to Skip and sent him up the hill with it. After you figured he was dead, you went after it, but it was covered with blood. You were too greedy not to take it, anyhow."

There was a long, sudden silence. The Filers had their rifles aimed at the lawmen. Tyler and Ethan weren't sure they could draw fast enough.

"Just get back," Percy said. "All of you."

Ethan was grim. "You're under arrest."

Maggie and Celia backed away with Billy. The lawmen stood transfixed, covered by the rifles.

For a long while there was a hush. Any second now the marshal and Tyler could be shot clean through.

"We're leaving town," Percy said. "But not without our money. So these ladies are going with us. We'll let 'em go when we're in the clear."

Peter turned to reach for Celia, about to grab her as a hostage. He leaned toward her, his eyes blazing.

But Celia swung the lantern back and then threw it forward, striking Peter in the chest. Peter roared as flame and glass burned his face and neck. Percy turned for just a second.

Tyler reached out and shoved Ethan aside, even as he drew his six-gun and jumped away. The rifles barked, striking Tyler on the right arm, but he pulled the trigger twice. Ethan was on one knee, drawing his six-gun and firing.

Percy jerked back, a bullet in his arm. Peter was hit on the shoulder and neck, but he worked another bullet in his rifle. They kept firing. Tyler fired twice, hitting Peter in the gut and

Percy in the chest. The Filers shrieked and stumbled backward. They fell and crawled about on the ground, trying to stay upright. Then they crumpled up in a heap and died.

Tyler caught his breath, pain in his arm, and he looked at Ethan, who hadn't been hit. They heard running feet and voices. Two men were carrying lamps, but the moonlight was casting plenty of light.

The doctor was with the crowd, and he shook his head and said, "Well, look at that, Marshal. Can't you two stay out of trouble?"

"How's Paxton?" Tyler asked.

"He'll make it. He has a hard head."

"And Skip?"

"Talking his fool head off right in front of a lot of witnesses. Seems it was Peter Filer who killed Jody."

"Ouch," Tyler said.

"Just hold still. Well, it went clean through. You come on over and let me clean it up for you."

Tyler nodded, turned, then paused. Celia and Maggie were standing there with Billy. Ethan stomped out the small fire burning in the oil as Maggie came forward and took his arm.

"Oh, Ethan."

"Don't worry, Maggie. It's over."

Then Ethan turned and put his hand on Tyler's shoulder. Father and son had a long moment of warmth as they thought ahead to a new life together. Abruptly, Ethan threw his arms around Tyler and hugged him. That hug made up for all the misery in Tyler's life.

As Ethan and Maggie turned away, Tyler had tears in his eyes. He watched them move through the crowd, Billy at their heels. The moon disappeared behind another cloud. The doctor turned and left with the onlookers, and now it was just Tyler and Celia, alone in the chill of night.

Tears were trickling down her face. "Oh, Tyler! I was so frightened. Thank God you're all right."

He swallowed, his hand on his bleeding arm.

She came closer, took his left arm, and started to guide him around the jail. "It's over now, isn't it?"

"Yeah, I reckon. But you took a big chance, throwing that lamp. You could have been shot."

"You and your father will be leaving."

"Yeah, but Maggie too, and Billy, and my pal Shorty. And you're part of the family."

"But I don't want to be your sister."

He paused in the moonlight, barely able to see the glow on her face. "I had something else in mind."

"Yes, Tyler?"

"How does Mrs. Tyler Mandell sound?"

"I like it."

She stood on her tiptoes as he bent his head, and she kissed him soundly, her fingers sliding up around his neck to hold him a long moment. It sent crazy shivers through him, and as he leaned back with his left arm around her, he grinned.

"Did you really miss that silver dollar?"

"You'll never know, will you, Tyler?"

And she laughed. It was a sweet, musical laugh that he would hear with joy for the rest of his life.

ABOUT THE AUTHOR

*W*estern novelist and screenwriter **Lee Martin** grew up on cattle ranches in Northern California. Martin began writing in the third grade and, later in life, wrote and sold 43 short stories before turning to novels with 23 now published. Martin is also a prolific writer of screenplays, mostly Westerns.

Martin's screenplay for *Shadow on the Mesa*, starring Kevin Sorbo, Wes Brown, and Gail O'Grady, was based on Martin's novel of the same title (Five Star Publishing, 2014). The movie was the second-highest-rated and second-most-watched original movie in Hallmark Movie Channel's history when it premiered in 2013. The film also won the prestigious Wrangler Award given by the National Cowboy & Heritage Museum in Oklahoma City for Best Original TV Western Movie.

Martin's recent novels, *The Grant Conspiracy*, *The Last Wild Ride*, and *Fury at Cross Creek*, all received rave reviews from *True West Magazine* and were based on Martin's screenplays, as is *Fast Ride to Boot Hill*. *In Mysterious Ways*, Martin's new modern suspense Western, received great critical acclaim from *Kirkus Reviews* and *Midwest Book Reviews*. *Trail of the Fast Gun* is the first book of seven in The Darringer Brothers series, all of which are reissued in paperback and ebook by Vaca Mountain Press.

Martin left the practice of law to write full-time, primarily concentrating on Western screenplays and novels, and often converting one to the other. Several of Martin's screenplays are currently under option by producers. To learn more, visit Lee Martin Westerns on Facebook.

Lee Martin